I Came Out For *This*?

Lisa Gitlin

Ann Arbor

D1444474

Copyright © 2010 by Lisa Gitlin

Bywater Books, Inc.
PO Box 3671
Ann Arbor MI 48106-3671
www.bywaterbooks.com

All rights reserved. No part of this book may be
reproduced or transmitted in any form or by any
means, electronic or mechanical, including photo-
copying, without permission in writing from the
publisher.

Printed in the United States of America on
acid-free paper.

Bywater Books First Edition: June 2010

Cover designer: Bonnie Liss (Phoenix Graphics)

ISBN 978-1-932859-73-7

This novel is a work of fiction. All persons and events
were created by the imagination of the
author.

This one's for you, Dad—
wherever you are . . .

I Came Out For *This?*

October 1999

All right, let's get the particulars out of the way for all you attentionally challenged freaks: My name is Joanna Kane. Jewish, 47, living in Cleveland, Ohio, which will prejudice you against me immediately because what's Cleveland, Ohio? A loser city. When you say you're from Cleveland, Ohio, people look at you with no expression, trying to think of what to say. Anyway, Joanna Kane, forty-seven, Jewish, living in pit stop on the lake. Professional fucking writer. Two parents, four siblings, no children because I never had a boyfriend or husband and I'm gay and was too stupid to come out until I was forty-five years old, so now I'm one of those aging pathetic spinsters that people feel sorry for, living in Cleveland, Ohio, that everyone laughs at. Typical history of troubles for a gay Jew. Was in a loony bin at age 14 for six months because I set fires to dumpsters and told my social worker at Child Guidance Clinic that I was going to blow up a gas station, so she put me in a bin. Not really crazy, just hiding my homosexuality and none of the stupid mental health people could figure it out. Attended Ohio University and moved to New York City to write. Ended up back in Cleveland after a mini-nervous breakdown, which I did not admit I was having. Have lived here for almost two decades and am sick of it, sick of my friends, sick of writing for the same boring publications and sick of being in this rut and will probably move to Washington, DC to be with Terri Rubin, who I hate.

I hate Terri Rubin, the woman I'm in love with, because she has put me in this hideous mood. I was in a perfectly good mood about a half-hour ago, and then she called and told me she's dating a woman named Sonya, who has an apothecary store in Bethesda, Maryland. What's an apothecary store, anyway? Doesn't it sound pretentious? I hate this Sonya and I hate Terri and I hate myself because I was never like this in my life. You know what it's like to come out when you're in your forties, having menopausal symptoms, for God's sake, and then fall madly in love with someone? All of a sudden you're in adolescence *for the first time.* You don't recognize yourself. I was a cool, collected writer who strutted around in jeans and a leather jacket, advising friends and siblings about their relationships, being a devoted daughter and a responsible professional person and a good citizen—well, except for not paying every dime of my taxes and having a couple DWIs—but you know, being pretty much on top of things, and then BAM! I realized I was gay and a couple months later, this sassy girl strutted into my life and I fell in love at first sight. After spending my life thinking that never really happened and only watching *West Side Story* because of the gangs. And then I became the kind of person I had always made fun of, who falls into a murderous rage because her beloved tells her she's dating some woman named Sonya, who has an apothecary store in Bethesda, Maryland. I'm sorry. I know I sound strident and . . . and . . . what's that word they always use to describe angry middle-aged woman? *Abrasive.* Yes. I'm sorry I'm being so *abrasive.* I'm just so upset. I'm just so upset. I don't know what to do anymore. For months I've just been sitting around in this apartment which used to be beautiful but I've let it go and it's filthy, and my cat died, and I'm not returning my friends' phone calls, and I pretty much stopped working because I couldn't write one more article about Life on the Streets or one more brochure for some airheaded nonprofit or one more newsletter for the Regional Sewer District—yes, I'm serious, I wrote about *sewers,* but I stopped doing that too. I'm done with everything. Friends, family, work, housekeeping. My bills are piling up. I don't even know why I'm writing this. But writers write, writers write, writers write. Writers are idiots. Submitting themselves to torture. For what?

I need to stop carrying on like this. Sonya will be history in two weeks. Terri never likes any of these women she dates. She is critical of everyone, including me. God knows what she tells people about me. She thinks I'm nuts because I fell so hard for her and won't let it go even though she keeps saying she only loves me as a friend. I suppose she figured when she came here last year to visit her parents that she would meet this friend of Willi's who just figured out she was gay, "initiate" her, and then gallivant back to DC and leave the little de-virginalized wretch to "move on." Move on! That's what everyone says. Well, Joanna, you need to MOVE ON! That's what

7

we do in this life! We get over our first big love and
MOVE ON! We accept the loss of our first big purple-
passion love, the one that made us burst like a rocket, the
one that made us howl at the moon, the one that turned
us into animals, and we MOVE ON and end up with a
more *mature* love that we stop fucking after about two
years and with whom our most exciting activity is discussing which cheese to purchase at the local Fancy
Foods. Well, fuck that. I don't want to move on. I've only
been young for two years. Why should I MOVE ON and
find some companion and spend the rest of my life eating
popcorn in front of the TV in my sock feet?

My mother just called right in the middle of this
tirade and I was mean to her. I dissed Cleveland. I called
it a pit stop. My mother thinks Cleveland is custard on a
stick, and carries on endlessly about the Cleveland
Orchestra and the Cleveland Playhouse and the beautiful
fall leaves and the adorable way Minnie Minoso, who
played for the Indians a million years ago, referred to
Cleveland as "Cleeblands." Now I feel bad. Maybe I
should call her back and apologize.

Oh, the hell with it. I'm going across the street and getting some flavored cigarettes. I only smoke when I drink,
and I'm going to drink. I feel like having a glass of the Chil-
ean red they have over at the new wine bar and a cherry-
flavored cigarette would taste real good with the wine. I'll
get a nice buzz and realize that Terri's dalliance with Sonya
what's-her-name is just a drop of piss in the wind.

That was a good idea. The wine settled me right down. I
do like that little bar on Coventry Road. I must have the

vestiges of alcoholism from when I was a young maniac whose life revolved around rum and cokes, because even though I don't drink that much anymore—well, maybe only once or twice a week—I still get that *thing* that alcoholics describe when I have my first drink, you know, like Oh, so *this* is real life, *this* is why I'm alive. And now I realize why I love Terri. Because she's so damn sexy with her sashaying walk, and because she's wickedly funny, she's affectionate and fun, she's out and proud, and most important, she has a sweet caramel-colored neck that compels me to kiss it every chance I get (she looks like a light-skinned black girl with her dusky skin and soft kinky hair, but she's really Jewish). I know that many people such as most of my friends and my sisters and brothers and her ex-lovers and a lot of *her* friends do not share my rapture over her and, in fact, think she's an evil bitch, but that's not a well-rounded assessment. (She would be very insulted if she read this. Maybe I should take it out.) See? This is the problem. I'm a wimp with her, always afraid of what she's going to think, and that's why she doesn't want me. Well, no, she doesn't want me because I'm not one of those trashy vamps in tight skirts and high heels, those high-femme women who Terri thinks are such hot babes but are really just neurotic whores. Most of those women aren't even gay anyway; they're just sick of men and are fooling around with women as a temporary distraction. I wonder if Sonya is like that.

But I digress. What I was saying was that I don't fit Terri's image of the ideal girlfriend. I'm on the femme side but I favor jeans and sensible shoes and I don't wear makeup except for lip gloss, and in my younger days people would tell me I looked like Mick Jagger, but now I just look like my mother. Anyway Terri is searching for someone different, someone who not only is a high-femme tart but who doesn't pour herself all over her like I did, but for God's sake, I was just coming out! I know I poured myself all over her, and then when she finally said she didn't want a relationship with me I hounded her like an overwrought child pursuing one of the Beatles, and now I regret behaving like such a ninny. But how absolutely divine it is, to experience your first love! I'll never forget the joy of meeting her. I was already all keyed up from having realized I was gay a few months before, and then Willi called and said her former social work volunteer that she'd been telling me about was in town and she arranged for us all to meet at the Mardi Gras Lounge and I walked in there with my friend Ann and this sexy Jewish girl sitting across from Willi flashed me a white-toothed grin and my outer layers just seared off. Even if I had known she was just seducing women to quell the pain of a broken heart, it wouldn't have made any difference. I blushed and giggled while she sat in the Mardi Gras with her arm draped over the booth behind me, flirting like mad, calling me a "hatchling" because I had just recently come out, picking up a lock of my hair and saying, "How can you *see* through all this?" She swaggered to the bathroom and I watched her sashaying butt in a grinning, stupid trance while Willi and Ann looked at me in amazement because they'd never seen me that way before. I asked her to go out to dinner with me and the next evening we went to a Chinese restaurant and afterwards

she kissed me in the car and suddenly I saw myself in
every romantic movie or ad or billboard, every song sung
by anyone named "Frankie" that I'd ever heard, and soon
thereafter she succumbed to my advances and I lay
naked in bed with her and ran my palm through her
coiled hairs and she whispered, "See how wet my pussy
gets when you touch me down there," and finally I knew
what the fuss was all about. Oh stop crying, Joanna.

I know Terri thinks I'm in la-la land. She's one of
these down-to-earth, practical people that would never
let herself get carried away like I did. But she *liked* that I
was in love with her, the wench. She *liked* that I wrote
her love letters saying that her breasts were like ripe
peaches, that I declared my love for her in this silly coming out piece I wrote for the local weekly paper, that I
wanted to move in with her two weeks after we met.
She just didn't count on my being so *persistent* about it,
didn't know I would call her in DC and nag her to let
me come and see her even though she told me she was
dating another woman, and when the woman didn't
work out and she broke down and invited me down
there for the 4th of July weekend I tumbled off the plane
all ga-ga over her and she was freaked out and kept me
at arm's length the whole time and told me it would
never work out between us and I flew home all smashed
up like roadkill.

After a couple weeks of sobbing I couldn't take it anymore, so I called her, and then she called me, and so it
went, and when she came back here in the fall to visit
her sick mother I was convinced she was here to visit *me*,
and I hung around her, mooning over her the whole

11

time. And then her mother died and instead of being properly sobered I continued to act like I was on speed, running down to visit her all the time to clutch and comfort her and have drunken sex that was tremendously exciting to me but for her was just an outlet for her grief.

The last time I visited her, which was this last summer, she told me before I came that she wanted me to sleep on the couch and I went anyway, and she was all lit up over this other woman and treated me like a beat-up table she meant to get rid of. But I refuse to let her go because I can't accept that I have ruined what is probably my only opportunity for love by being so naïve and stupid. I keep calling her, and she calls me too and tells me awful things like she's dating some woman who runs an apothecary store, and now I may just have to move there already. The hell with what my friends think. They all would be perfectly thrilled to see me go back to being that robot that I was before I came out, that marched around spouting my little philosophies and getting over-involved in their lives like some meddling auntie, and writing short stories that no one could relate to, like the one about an elderly couple with a pet fly. I didn't know beans about anything people would want to read about like love and romance or even sex because I always just faked it with all the men that had the misfortune to go to bed with me (although I must say in my own defense that I gave a very mean TOO MUCH INFORMATION! all right), but my point is that I wasn't a total drip. But I sure as hell am a drip now, sitting here on this blue couch for months, not returning phone calls and hardly ever working and being two months behind on my rent and thank God for Albert, my sweet old Cuban landlord, for not throwing me out of here. I can't stay here and I'm afraid to leave. I'm terrified to go to DC because what would I tell people? What would I tell *her*? I know you don't want me, but I'm moving there to be with you anyway, heh heh? I could *kill* her for ruining my life. Well, not ruining it but throwing a wrench in it. I was all set to move to DC and turn my life into an adventure again, which it has not been since I left New York City because I just stayed here like a slug instead of moving back there where I belong or at least becoming a war correspondent, but then Terri came along and I thought I was saved not only from a loveless life but from being stuck in the *antithesis* of a city that anyone wants to write about. And then she yanked away that string of goodies that she dangled before me—just pulled it back out of my reach and now I'm ruined. You can live with deprivation, but dashed expectations are a killer. It's not the desert that will do you in but the mirage. And fuck her anyway, lording it over my destiny, like the wizard spewing smoke and saying, "Take your broom and go away!" Or whatever it was he said, after poor Dorothy risked life and limb on that treacherous journey.

I miss my cat. I think I subconsciously let her die because I knew I couldn't leave Cleveland while I still had her. I bought some cheap carpet that only cost two hundred dollars, and the gases from it killed my cat. I should have gotten rid of the carpet as soon as I saw her never lying on it and always wanting to be outdoors after I bought it. She got some kind of cancer and died, I'm assuming from being driven out of her home. I used to be a nice nurturing person and now I'm a selfish distracted child who can't even care for her own cat.

 This wine is wearing off. What should I do now? I wonder if that egg salad is still any good.

November 1999

I'm being carried down the rapids. This idea that we are
the captain of our fates is ridiculous because when you're
in the rushing river what are you supposed to do—turn
around? You can't. I gave Albert notice and I'm moving
out of this apartment in two weeks. I've already started
to pack, and you should see this place. It's disgusting. I'm
wallowing in dust here; I'm in a diaphanous world of dust.
I'm being carried down the rushing rapids and I'm in a
diaphanous world of dust at the same time. How can you
be two places at once when you're really nowhere at all?
(Remember that line from *Firesign Theatre*?)

I'm going to put my stuff in storage and stay upstairs
at Tommy's until I move to DC. Everyone is saying, "But
Terri's in DC," as though they were saying, "But that's
where the cholera epidemic is." Willi, who is kind of
upset that she introduced me to Terri, especially because
she used to be my therapist, said resignedly, "Well, maybe
you have to put yourself in the lion's mouth." But I'm
already *in* the lion's mouth so I might as well be in the
lion's mouth down *there*. The problem is, I have no money
and no job and no place to live and nobody just *moves*

17

to Washington, DC. They go down there after they get some *position*. But I'll figure it all out, because once I set my mind to something, I find a way to do it. Don't I? I think I do.

My younger sister Queen (a nickname; she calls me Peeps) is the one who nudged me into the rapids. I was visiting her in Toledo last week, and we were sitting in our favorite coffee shop, surrounded by leering paper pumpkins, and I was babbling about What should I do, what should I do? Finally she said, "You just need to go." And that was it. That decided it. *I just need to go.* It's better to be in the rushing river than to sit and stare at the froth day after day. So here I am, being carried along, and I'm feeling all pumped up except when I remember that I haven't even told Terri yet. That's right, I've started to pack my things and I'm checking newspaper ads for storage facilities and places to stay in DC and I haven't told Terri I'm coming. She was on vacation for two weeks, so I couldn't call her, but she's been back for two days and I keep putting it off. But I am going to call her today. In fact, I'm going to call her now. I'm going to stop writing and call her.

The thing is, I don't know what to tell her. I feel as though I'm disrespecting her, like I don't believe her that she doesn't want a relationship with me. I used to hate it when men I had turned away continued to call me and would leave twenty messages a day on my machine, or banged on my door unannounced. It infuriated me, in fact. It seemed so . . . so . . . presumptuous. And here I am, acting just like them. But it's not as though she's the only reason I'm moving there, I'm leaving for other reasons, and I should at least give myself a chance to be in the same city with her. We've never lived in the same city before, going about our daily business, without some melodrama occurring every second. I can't just stay here, poaching in my own juices while she cozies up to a woman who runs an apothecary store. Sometimes she exasperates me. She's so stodgy and unimaginative. She bases all her conclusions on cold, hard facts and fails to see *possibilities*. I always see possibilities. I can make champagne out of sour lemons. Terri would say, "You can only make sour lemonade from sour lemons," but what does she know about alchemy? She is Dionysian, of the earth, and I am Apollonian, of the sky, and only I have the perspective to see that transformative place where earth and sky meet. She can't see it because she's down there stuck in the mud.

Oh please, Joanna. Stop your blithering and call her.

Well, now I feel kind of jerky. I essentially lied to her. I told her I've decided to move to DC because I'm in a rut and I need to be in a more cosmopolitan city and that Washington, DC is my second-favorite city after New York, all of which is true. But then I said that I've worked through my feelings for her and I've decided I can handle living in proximity to her and we can be friends. And while I was saying that, I felt like about a million miles away from my own treacherous mouth. And then I went back into myself and said truthfully that I hoped she wasn't upset by this news and then *she* lied and said, "Not at all! It will be nice to have more 'family' here." So there we were, babbling on top of the real issues the way we always do because I don't face the facts and she tries to process everything mentally and ignore the turmoil inside of her. But I'm sure she's plenty discombobulated and is probably conveying my news in urgent tones to Tiny or Linda as we speak, and you can bet your bippy she'll have a nice juicy session with her therapist on Friday.

So here I am, hightailing off to the country's most bloodthirsty city to win the heart of a woman who has tossed me away like a supermarket mailer. My friend Tommy and I laugh hysterically at this image we've concocted of me suffering some final, devastating rejection by her and running naked and shrieking down Connecticut Avenue and ending up in a nuthouse or some cult for melt-down people. Like my mother would say in Yiddish, "Nitoh ver tsu lachn!"—"There's nobody to laugh." Loosely translated, it means, It's not even funny.

It really isn't funny. I'm so scared. But you know what? Underneath my terror is the conviction that I'm doing the right thing. I suppose it's because I feel as though I'm doing something normal, for a change. Not that it's considered totally sane to run off to some city in pursuit of someone who has rejected you, but at least it's being crazy in a normal way, instead of being crazy in a crazy way like I've done all my life, setting trash fires and riding a moped around Harlem at night and writing short stories about people with pet flies and eating mayonnaise from the jar and acting like an overall general weirdo that everyone thinks is so cute but is really just sick. This is the kind of crazy thing that lots of people do. And now I'm doing it too.

So after all is said and done, that's why I've decided to move to DC. Because it makes me feel like part of humanity.

There. I figured it all out.

December 1999

I love myself! I've never done anything like this before, the kind of thing that if someone else did it I would think it was so cool. Five hours ago, I jumped into my 15-year-old hoopty and tore out of Cleveland, leaving my whole draggy life back there. Tommy grumpily helped me pack the car with a bunch of clothes and my computer, and I hugged him good-bye and took off like a thief in the night. Nobody else even knows I'm gone except for my parents because you can't just not tell my mother something. So here I am in an EconoLodge in Breezewood, PA, a constellation of motels and eateries near the Maryland border, and I have the same current of excitement running through me as I had when I was 21 and moved to New York. It's partly because it was the same time of year as now; it was cold and the air was heavy and had that peppery, metallic smell.

I haven't just run off like some teenager, by the way. I have found a job and a place to stay in DC. The job is the best part. I'm going to be a field interviewer for a government health study. I'm taking a step down from writing for a living and I don't care because I never liked writing for other people and only did it because I'm a Jewish girl from a middle-class community, and in spite of my rebel image I always thought I should be some sort of "professional." I have no desire to do "communications" in Washington DC and deal with stuffy DC bureaucrats that wear navy suits and use phrases like "intellectual capital" and exude arrogance to hide their rage about being nobodies in big fat Washington. This field interviewing job will allow me to be more like the free-wheeling journalist I actually am, bopping around the city, getting people to talk to me.

I am a little nervous about the place that I found to stay in, a rooming house that ran an ad in the DC gay newspaper, which I responded to and was told by the manager that I could have my own, small room with a shared bath for just $250 per month. I almost fell over when I heard the price and asked him to please hold the room for me. But when I hung up and told Tommy about it, he said that for $250 per month my "find" was obviously some queer flophouse, implying that it was one of those Bowery-type places with cracked cement floors and metal beds with sagging mattresses and men spitting up hockers in the halls and blowing one another in the "shared bathrooms." I think Tommy is just trying to freak me out because he's pissed off that I'm going to Washington and abandoning him, but what if I show up at this place tomorrow and it *is* like that? I would die before calling Terri to rescue me, especially since she agrees with Tommy that I shouldn't go there. I suppose I'll have to go out to Rockville and stay with Willi's cousin Marj, which is so far out of the city it would be like staying somewhere in Iowa.

Well, that's not going to happen anyway. It's probably some charming, weather-beaten mansion with a big front porch and original woodwork and vintage carpeting. Right now, I'm not going to let anybody's Gloomy Gus predictions fuck up my rhythm. I feel the future roaring through me like a locomotive! I love motels. This EconoLodge is adorable, with its faux early-American decor. I know I could have left earlier and driven straight through, but I like doing things at night and also I wanted to savor this move, turn it into a mini-road trip. So now I'm Jack Kerouac for a night. Go, man, go! (Actually, Kerouac annoyed me. He thought he was so hip, but really he was a flag-waving conservative who couldn't roll with the sixties and ended up as a flabby, drunken recluse in his mother's house while the rest of the world was out raising hell.) But tonight I will savor the myth of *On the road* without dwelling on grim postscripts.

I'm very nervous about seeing Terri, but right now it's a good nervous, like salt on your tongue—the high-quality kosher salt with coarser grains that my mom uses in her vegetable soup. I like this kind of nervous—the stimulating kind. It's the *other* kind of nervous that I hate, the kind that's more like inhaling sulfur, the kind that nauseates me and slows me down. In general, I don't mind being nervous, because it's my natural state. It's when I'm *not* nervous that I start to worry.

Ha, ha. That was funny, right? I am my own most appreciative audience. I'd better go to sleep. It's 2 a.m. I don't function well on no sleep. But I'm over-excited. I'll probably be awake until four. What if I'm late getting

27

there tomorrow and that guy gives away my room? Well, I suppose I shouldn't care, if it's one of those places with saggy mattresses and cement floors and semen stains. But I don't think it will be like that. I think it will be perfectly nice.

I am in heaven. Imagine Washington, DC being heaven. But I'm lying on a single bed in a tiny room with two large, sun-streaming windows letting in what feels like a semi-tropical breeze. That's right. It's 70° in Washington, DC in the middle of December. When the manager of this place showed me this room with these big old windows, I almost swooned with relief. I can live anywhere with big bright windows. I would rather live in a closet with big bright windows than in a dark mansion. I wouldn't want to live in a mansion anyway. But this is fantastic, lying on this single bed that reminds me of lying in my little bed at home when I was sick and I could hear the shouts of the kids coming home from school through the open windows, just like now, except back in those days they weren't cursing.

The rooming house itself is perfectly habitable. It's clean, quiet, and shows no evidence of debauchery. Actually it's not a "house" at all, but rather a small, red-brick building. It used to be a halfway house for women prisoners, but a couple years ago the city closed the place and sold the building to a skinny, nervous gay guy who turned it into a residence for queers. The building is very plain, but it's on a block full of renovated row houses painted in lovely southern colors like peach, avocado, and sky blue, and it's just a block from U Street, which is the hot new strip in DC. When I looked at the map, I realized that this neighborhood is right next to Dupont Circle, where Terri lives, and it's an easy walk. When I saw how close I was to her, it kind of freaked me out.

My room is on the second floor in the back of the house, where I have plenty of privacy. It's tiny and cozy, with blue walls and brown carpeting, a single bed with a blue-green comforter, a white dresser and matching night stand, and two big windows, one facing east and the other facing south. There's even a little TV on the dresser, with cable. The bathroom is right outside my door, and although I have to share it with two other people, I have not yet seen them. The only two residents I've met so far are a sweet white swishy kid about eighteen and a big guy with a marbled face from one of those pigment deficiencies. They were in the dumpy little living room downstairs watching a huge TV when Russell, the manager, was showing me around the house yesterday.

I did have one experience that reminded me of how irritating DC can be. Yesterday after I unloaded my stuff, Russell, an engaging, mischievous queer with mocha skin and wild, brillo pad hair, took me under his wing. He had me ride with him to pick out Christmas trees for him and his "Aunt" Ethel, who lives across the street from him, and after we got the trees and dumped them in his back yard he asked me if I wanted to go to a holiday party given by the Shaw–U Street neighborhood association.

The party was in a fine old U Street bar, and we walked over there and met Russell's brother Mikey and Aunt Ethel, a sweet black lady in her seventies. As soon as we sat down at a back table, I noticed that almost all the other people in the room were white. I thought this was weird since Shaw–U Street, although gentrifying, is still an overwhelmingly black neighborhood, and in fact was once known as DC's "black Broadway" because of all the famous entertainers who performed in clubs here. We got our buffet food, and while we ate I watched all these whiteys in their crisp outfits sporting their little name tags marching around with their plates full of broccoli, and finally I leaned over and asked Miss Ethel, "Who *are* these people?" and she replied, "Well, I don't really know any of them." I was very taken aback, thinking that in Cleveland, which is a very grassroots town with a big working class, a respectable lady like Miss Ethel (who has lived in this neighborhood her whole life) would be a *leader* in her community organization; they would have gone out and *recruited* her. But DC has only privileged white people (like me, but I don't count because I'm a starving writer) and they're all so oblivious. After we ate our buffet meal, they set up a microphone and started making speeches about "How far we've come and how far we have to go" while the black people just huddled around the fringes. At one point, a very big woman in tan pants and a yellow blazer walked over and stood with her ass almost in Miss Ethel's face while she talked to a lady at the next table, and Miss Ethel just moved her chair a little, didn't even make a face or any kind of wisecrack. I assumed that Miss Ethel was just one of those black southern aristocrats who is above laughing at white people, but Russell and Mikey weren't laughing, either. DC is such a goody-two-shoes town, and I guess I'll have to get used to it, but I can't stand seeing straight white people riding roughshod over everyone else in the most cavalier way, making the other people feel like little nothings and hate themselves. It happened to me and it practically ruined me. Although I have to admit that there were some gay white boys at that event and they were acting even worse than the straight white people.

I hate to say it, but Terri fits right into hoity-toity DC. She's such a good, example-setting lesbian, with her career as a "diversity trainer" and her reputation in the gay community as a political advocate and her involvement in lesbo "leadership activities" that are the equivalent of Hadassah for Jewish ladies. I, on the other hand, am a bad lesbian who listens to macho music, including rap and makes fun of lesbos who sing sorrowful songs at coffee houses and says sarcastic things about women who are afraid to come out. So how can we possibly get along?

The answer is that Terri is only a goody-goody on the surface. Her real self is very spicy. I can tell you this: If some woman stuck her ass in her face, that wench wouldn't just sit there and take it. She would tap the woman on the shoulder and when the woman turned around she would say with a little smile, "If I wanted your ass in my face I would have asked for it."

I really need to let her know I'm here. I wonder if she'll be happy that I'm living practically next door to her.

I'm kind of nervous to call her. I feel as though I need to get a little more settled. Maybe I'll give her a ring tomorrow, or at least on Monday. If I wait too long, she'll be pissed.

Well, I finally saw my little peppercorn. Just as I predicted, she was irritated that I waited three days to call her. It's not that she couldn't wait to see me, God forbid that should be the case; it's just that she likes to *know* everything, and my traipsing around DC for three days without her knowledge violated her notion of what's right and proper. But when she said, "Come over now!" I was as ecstatic as if she had just asked me to marry her.

But then, walking to her new condo in Dupont Circle, I passed her old place, a glowering building on 15th Street, where I was always trying to kiss her ass and nothing I did was ever right and I got stuck on the elevator and she accused me of deliberately making us miss our play and once, I walked outside after I'd been crying and a toddler in his mom's arms pointed at me and said, "Grandma!" and I walked to my car feeling like an old lady and found a ticket on it, and when all that came back to me that same mood enveloped me and I started to wonder why I even moved here to be tortured by this ridiculous relationship.

And then I got to her building on Q Street off of 19th and looked up at her second-floor window, and my panic had a chemical reaction and suddenly I was surging with lust. Terri buzzed me up and opened the door wearing her jeans and checkered shirt, with her kinky salt-and-pepper hair cut short and a fresh tan from a recent trip to the Caribbean. She didn't smile or light up when she saw me—ironically, she always accuses *me* of not looking happy to see *her*, and once even said I looked as though I had gallstones which, it turns out, I actually do—but she hugged me long and hard and emotionally, and I cried. Her mother's death still hangs in the air between us, intensifying everything.

Terri's place is what decorators might call "well appointed"—the living room, more of a parlor, contains a loveseat, an old china cabinet, a rag rug, and plants decorating a large window, the bedroom is spacious and modern, the kitchen and bathroom are spotless, and the whole place has the same lemony-fresh scent that was in her 15th Street apartment, which frankly made me a little sick from the association.

She had prepared a plate of hors d'oeuvres for us and we went into the bedroom to eat them and share a bottle of wine. The first thing she told me is that she got rid of that Sonya person with the apothecary store. She said the woman got too clingy. Everyone is always too clingy for her. In the past year, she's gotten rid of about six women who supposedly were too clingy. She even thought I was too clingy, which was a lie because I am not at all clingy. Actually the word she used was "cloying." When she told me I was "cloying," I almost killed her.

Really. She's lucky to still be alive after saying that to me. But I'm sure all the other ones really were too clingy.

Lying in bed next to the wench, I felt like someone whose estranged family has let her into the foyer but hasn't decided whether to allow her back into the house. I so wanted to start ripping her clothes off. Sometimes her clothes irritate me because they're *on* her. It's not as though they're so fashionable or anything. I wanted to tear off those shabby old moccasins and throw them across the room and tear off her shirt and stamp on it and pull her pants off and hurl them out the window and then start *ravaging* her, to bite her lips and nip at her neck and inhale her skin and shove her breasts in my mouth and then make my way south to the jungle and have myself a wild feast. Terri has such an organic taste, like wild berries—in contrast with the couple of other women I've been with, one of whom sprayed something down there, which made her taste like orange potpourri that you buy at the dollar store.

But I couldn't attack her because she's doing this "friend" thing. I just had to lie there like a big sister and listen to her recite every detail of her day: she discovered a spot on her mother's rug and she took her car in for an oil change and she talked to Ruby, her mom's former housekeeper, on the phone. She likes to report everything that happens to her and I hang onto every word, even though in general I have little patience for minutiae and if someone else reported every detail of their life I would be secretly furious at having to listen to them. (I even stopped being friends with my friend Shelly when she moved into her condo and started obsessing about her countertops and silverware drawer, and then she got a brain tumor and died and I still feel guilty whenever I think about how I abandoned her.)

While I was there, the phone rang and it was the head of some nominating committee asking Terri to give a speech on behalf of her Congressional candidate. Terri said the candidate was a secret dyke and all the dykes are rooting for her and Terri had lunch with her and confronted her about being a secret dyke and the woman refused to come out to her. Terri said she will refuse to give the speech. She said she found the woman "off-putting." Terri can be arbitrary, which isn't always pleasant, but I like her unwavering stand on political issues. She's actually somewhat famous in DC as a gay advocate and has been quoted in newspapers and even had an article written about her.

The two of us are so goofy. We were lying around getting drunk and she looked at me and said, "Knadel," (she calls me Knadel) "you have a bug on your head." And I said, "I do not! What are you talking about?" And she reached over and picked something out of my hair and it was a ladybug! In the middle of winter! And I said, "You put it there." And she said. "Why would I put a bug on your head?" And I said, "Just to embarrass me." And she said, "Honey, I don't have to do anything to embarrass you. You do that well enough on your own." And I said, "Give me that ladybug! I want it. A ladybug is good luck." I grabbed her hand and she flicked off the ladybug and it flew away. I said, "I bet it's your little pet." And she said, "That's right. It's my magic bug." And I said, "It's *my* magic bug. It wanted to be in *my* hair." And she said,

"That's because it misses being outside in the dirt." And I slapped her and said, "My hair is very clean." And so it went.

But underneath all our banter was tension you could cut with a knife. It was the tension of two people who care about each other but have also driven each other nuts. It was floating there like a body that girls levitate at a sleep-over. You know, that game when you make someone lie on the floor and gather around her and chant that she's getting lighter and lighter and suddenly you lift her way up and start screaming. So there I was with Terri and this levitated body was scarily floating there and we just ignored it and kept babbling at each other.

Now I'm back home in my teeny little room and the wine is wearing off and the levitated body has drifted in here. It's making me nervous. What if things don't work out between us, now that I've gone and moved here? What will I do? But they have to. I can't envision any other conclusion. I think my whole problem right now is that I haven't eaten anything all day except for two of those appetizers that Terri made. I'm starting to feel weak and vulnerable. I can just hear my mother: "*Shame on you! What kind of a person goes all day without eating? You're just too lazy to get up off your fanny and walk to Benny's Chili Bowl!*" That's what she calls Ben's Chili Bowl, the famous eatery on U Street, which has served the likes of Bill Cosby and Denzel Washington. I think I do need to go to "Benny's Chili Bowl" and get a chili dog. That will be like a tiger in my tank.

I wonder if I'm hypoglycemic.

Yesterday I decided to go to a monthly lesbian potluck that was advertised in the *Blade*. (Since I came out, I've gotten the impression that lesbians are obsessed with potlucks.) The potluck was on 17th Street, which is DC's main gay strip, above a Greek restaurant. I walked over with my famous deviled eggs and the hostess, a stylish African-American woman named Dee, was sweetly enthusiastic when I presented them. Her place was impeccable, with tribal art on the walls, masks and small drums and primitive paintings, and her furniture was basic but nicely arranged and comfortable. The room, which contained fewer than a dozen women, was charged with that unnerving combination of anxiety and controlled lust/need that is more pronounced among women than among men and women. Lesbians are terrified to talk to one another, but when they do, they snap together like legos.

The apartment was larger than it looked at first. When I walked into the kitchen, I noticed a cozy den off of it, and three women were in there, drinking and laughing loudly. Then I noticed this electric punch bowl on the kitchen counter with punch cascading into it. Lesbo functions are often BYOB or dry, but considering the demeanor of the three women, this punch was spiked. Charmed by our hostess' generosity, I filled a class and shyly wandered into the den.

An hour and three drinks later, the three laughing women were my best friends. I especially connected with Bette, a little busty blond firecracker who told us a hilarious coming-out story that involved her boyfriend discovering her and the family doctor in a compromised position on the doctor's examining table. A tall, square-jawed Bostonian named Jean said she'd never been with a man and couldn't even imagine it, and I said, "When I think of how many times I actually fucked them, I can't even believe it," and we were getting drunker and drunker and pretty soon we were screaming with laughter. A gorgeous brunette named Pia in her early thirties, whose sweetness seemed incongruous with her siren good looks, said that she had a girlfriend who went back to men and now she's an Avon lady, and for some reason this struck us as funny too. Every once in a while, Dee came back and asked us if we needed anything, and even though we kept telling her we were fine with the vodka punch she brought in a plate of cheese and crackers and said, "Here, crazy ladies, try some solids," and then she swished back out.

After a while, Dee came back and said everyone else had left, and I suggested that we help clean up and she said, "Absolutely not. There's not that much to do and I can deal with it tomorrow." Then Bette suggested going down the street to a historic restaurant down the street that had a bar down in the cellar. Everyone including Dee was up for it, so the five of us traipsed down the street to this place and down some stone steps and burst into the bar like a street gang. Even Dee had a great time, although the rest of us were already loaded and she wasn't, so she kind of exchanged looks with the bartender, as though to say, "I feel your pain." We started ordering drinks and smoking Jean's Virginia Slims, and we were yelling on top of one another and creating a commotion while the bald, macho-looking bartender served us with bartenderly forbearance. Bette insisted that we all go upstairs to see the stately old rooms (the restaurant was closed), and I imagined them filled with people in their 19th-century finery, the men in their vests and suspenders and the women in their dresses stiffened by petticoats, and I was ecstatic to be experiencing DC just as *myself*, Joanna Kane, who knows how to navigate through the world. I've always had friends. Even when I was a little kid that grown-ups didn't like because I was a bit sullen, I got along with other kids, with whom I made up games like Wicked Spirits and Round the Mulberry Bush and tore through the neighborhood on a Murray bicycle. I even reluctantly conceded to playing "dolls" with my best friend Karen (who, incidentally, is *still* my best friend), and although I sneered that I hated dolls I got so involved in our play-acting that I would have to be torn away when Karen's mom called us for dinner.

Today Terri called and when I told her I'd been to the potluck, which she knew about but didn't feel like going, she asked if I met anyone I would want to date. I was kind of hurt, and if I had any smarts I would have suggested that I *had* met someone, like the fetching Dee, for example. But I am a very bad liar, and in fact, I compulsively tell everybody everything. I used to be so close-mouthed and secretive, and then I came out and now I spew everything that pops into my head. But who cares that Terri knows what I did last night? It was still *my* thing, which had nothing to do with her. I feel as though my life in DC didn't start when I went over to Terri's. It started when I was sitting in that room drinking and laughing and just being me, the "me" that makes friends as easily as switching on a light. It's always been that way. I may have been lonely over the years, but I've always had people around me.

I've been doing my field interviewing job for two weeks. I get paid to drive all over DC, blasting my radio and going to randomly selected addresses and interrogating people about their health. The supervisor, an obsessive middle-aged woman who thinks this health study is the salvation of humanity, is already singing my praises because I can slip into locked buildings with my charm and my unobtrusiveness and my middle-aged white femaleness, and I can get people to talk to me because I am a writer and know how to extract information from people, and I am a Jewish girl and don't mind being kind of naggy about it.

I drive around the city with emotions ripping through me, shifting constantly between excitement and nervousness and hope and embarrassment that I was such a damn fool to come here. This whole city reminds me of Terri—its power-tripping and preoccupation with "doing the right thing" and its political correctness overlying a kind of animal ruthlessness. And, like Terri, DC is physically impressive, although unlike her, it is not sexy. DC is probably the least sexy city in the world. But

I feel more sexually alive here than I have felt anywhere else. It's ridiculous. Why couldn't she have lived in New York or San Francisco or some more romantic city? Then this whole adventure might feel a little less bizarre.

I only knew a sliver of DC before, the Northwest quadrant, where Terri and I live and which contains the white neighborhoods and the touristy areas like Dupont Circle and Georgetown and Embassy Row on Massachusetts Avenue. Tourists are led to believe that DC consists of Northwest DC and Capitol Hill, and the rest of the city is hidden away like a demented old aunt who might remove her bloomers in the middle of the book club meeting. But now that I'm a field worker I have gotten to know Northeast DC with its hodgepodge of shabby projects and duplex-lined streets and sprawling institutions that make it hard to navigate, and notorious Southeast DC with its gangs and guns and stately old homes, and Southwest DC on the riverfront with its blocky modern apartment buildings that make it look like Soviet Russia.

I got mugged last night and it was all my fault. I was standing on Bladensburg Road in this Northeast slum called Trinidad, trying to figure out where this street was, and a derelict sauntered up to me and offered to help, and instead of losing him like a sensible person I started to blither at him about looking for this street, and all of a sudden he pointed a pocket knife at me and demanded my money. I gave him ninety dollars, which I had withdrawn from the bank and forgot to leave at home, and he staggered away. The funny thing was that I wasn't really scared of the mugger, but I was scared *afterwards*, of Terri finding out about it. In my humiliation and upset, I was sure she would judge me as harshly as I judged myself, that she would think I was stupid for walking around a slum with ninety dollars and then talking to a derelict as though he were my Aunt Bessie. I was afraid she would consider me a burden and withdraw from me. Of course, this isn't true—most likely she would be very sympathetic—but I'm not going to tell her anyway. I know it's ridiculous to be more scared of some woman who makes tapas for you when you come to her house than of a mugger with a knife. But when you really think about it, who is really more dangerous, a scrawny little mugger or someone you're in love with? I rest my case.

Yesterday was Friday and Terri invited me to an evening movie at the Uptown Theater in Cleveland Park. It was the first time we ever went to the movies together and it felt so datey, and I wore my green sweater and my high black shiny boots. I walked to her place, and when I showed up at her door she looked at the boots and said, "Ooh, baby, put me on my *knees!*" That gave me a rush, although I tried to be cool. The movie was this silly *Stuart Little* that *she* wanted to see, about a mouse that's adopted by a human family, and I prefer hard-edged movies about gun-toting street children, but I enjoyed it because it took place in my beloved New York and this mouse ends up having all kinds of funky, back-alley adventures. During the movie, I couldn't resist running my hands through her soft woolly hair, and I know she liked it because her face softened and she sat real still.

Afterwards we went to a Vietnamese restaurant that has the most delicious summer rolls, and I ate everything to please her—the summer rolls, the spicy eggplant, and the bean curd with ginger sauce. She takes food very seriously and I always let her order when we eat out. She complains that I eat like a bird, but it's not true; it's just that sometimes when I'm with her I'm too nervous to eat. I'm too nervous to do anything properly. For example, during our meal I remarked that my chopsticks looked strange and Terri looked at them and pointed out that I was holding them upside-down. She laughed uproariously and even though I laughed too I was really furious at myself because she already has this image of me as some bumbling space cadet, which I'm not.

While we were eating, she told me that her brother in Ohio told her he thought it took "guts" for me to move here. She was implying that her brother admired me for moving here in defiance of everyone, including her. I think she was fishing for some indication of how I still felt about her. I could have said, "Yeah it took guts, and I'm not through yet," or *something* to indicate that I'm still sweet on her. But I just smiled and said, "Oh, really?" I suppose she doesn't know if I'm still in love with her, and it bothers her. I'm propelled by my intuition, but she's propelled by knowledge; without *knowing* something, she loses her bearings. Even though she thinks she's already decided that I'm not "The One," she would still want to know if I still love her. And how can she know, when I haven't told her? I have this old habit of assuming people know how I feel because my feelings are so potent, roiling around inside of me. But in reality I'm harder to read than most people.

We took the train back to Dupont Circle and I walked with her to her apartment, but then she said she was tired and she hoped I didn't mind this time if she didn't invite me in. The tentacles of pain started reaching for me. But then she kissed me goodbye on the mouth and the garlic on her breath caressed me like the first soft gust of spring. She said jauntily, "I'm glad you're here, Knadel!" Then she grinned and turned and sauntered into her building. I walked home and got undressed and got into bed and I realized I was horny as hell. I snatched up my vibrator and tried to summon up my prison warden fantasy, but then Terri burst in and before I could stop her she was fucking me with her "lady luck" dildo, whispering obscenities in my ear. I have resolved to keep her out of my fantasies until I can have her again in reality, but last night there was nothing I could do—she just swaggered into my S&M scene and took over, bumping aside my beloved prison warden.

But today I'm a little depressed because Terri didn't invite me in last night. I keep thinking it's because I held my chopsticks upside-down. It's so ridiculous, but I keep thinking about it, and then I think that Terri is right to not want such a silly ass who obsesses about chopsticks, and then I go right back to thinking about it. Do most people have such ridiculous thoughts when they're almost fifty years old? I know people do have ridiculous thoughts when they're in love. But I'm wondering if I'm being even more ridiculous and obsessive than most people who are in love. Isn't this what children do when they're about thirteen? I didn't. When I was thirteen, I was a tough little customer. "But I was so much older then . . . I'm younger than that now." Dylan said that.

I feel a bit sheepish to admit this, but it turns out that my rooming house does have characteristics of a deviant flophouse. Even though physically it's clean and well-kept, the residents are all wacko. Of course, I have become friends with all of them. Like Willi says, I have no boundaries.

I've started to wonder if even I am too normal for this place. Today I was lying on my bed reading when Johnny, a DC native with an outdated "fade" hairstyle and pant legs the size of laundry sacks burst into my room to complain about his boyfriend, Guillermo, a sweet, pockmarked Bolivian kid. He said Guillermo had gotten mixed up with a bunch of neighborhood thugs, and not only was he fucking them but he was running around with them on thieving expeditions, ripping off stores and then returning the items using homemade receipts. A minute later Guillermo burst in, yelling, "Joanna, don't listen to him! Everything he says is a lie!" And then he yelled at Johnny, "Why are you telling Joanna about the receipts and making me look bad? Anyway, who was with us yesterday when we bought the chicken wings with money we got from taking back the porcelain pig?" I couldn't get a word in edgewise because they kept screaming at each other and eventually they left, continuing their fight all the way down the hall.

People seem to have sticky fingers around here, I guess because they're all poor. If you put a sandwich in the fridge, it's gone an hour later. A few days ago I found these two druggie-looking queens, who live in a room in the basement, rooting through the mail. I wondered who the hell would send them mail, but I just took my mail and went back upstairs, and then I left my room to go to work and I ran into Jerome, a strapping, coal-black sex worker whom I've become friendly with. He asked me if I wanted to share a pizza, and I said I had to go to work, and at that moment the seedy queens, Ginger and Calliope, came marching up the stairs with a Pizza Hut box, followed by Donald, a rotund tenant who works in a men's clothing store. Donald was screaming, "I know you stole my credit card from the mail to order that damn pizza. And y'all didn't even have the decency to offer me any!" I just pushed past them and went downstairs.

When I came home from work, I paid Jerome a visit and found him cooing at someone over the phone, in a buttery, Barry White voice, that he's going to "split their tender peaches" and "curl their toes." He smiled at me when I walked in and made his date and got off the phone. I said, "Did you all order pizza with Donald's credit card that Ginger and Calliope stole from the mail?" Jerome waved my question away and said, "Don't worry about that faggot. He owed me some money anyway. Trust me." Jerome is always saying, "Trust me." Then he said, "I gave him back his damn credit card."

This place is teaming with nut cases. There are a couple of respectable working men here, like Donald, and Tomas, a courteous Brazilian attaché who stays in his room all the time, but it seems I have gotten more involved with the crazies. My most normal friend here is Russell, the house manager, who comes over every day, acting like a cross between a maid and a resident advisor, vacuuming and cluttering around in the kitchen and gossiping with all the tenants, many of whom he knows, shall we say, intimately.

Leave it to me to become a den mother to a houseful of delinquents while every other middle-aged lesbo in this town is living in some house or apartment by herself or with a girlfriend or nice tame roommate. I haven't invited Terri over here yet, but I can't put it off forever. God knows what she'll think of my little haven. Maybe I can make everyone stay in their rooms when she comes. I'm just kidding. If she doesn't like my new buddies, tough beans. It's not as though she's never done drugs or fucked her brains out or lived in a funky house. I'm sure she would say, "I've never stolen or smoked crack or prostituted myself," in her snooty voice that I can't stand. But then again, how can she not approve of an affordable rooming house for gay people?

She probably would approve of such a place. Unless *I'm* in it. If *I'm* in it, she'll find some derogatory thing to say about it. I have to admit, though, there's plenty of grist for her mill.

Today I woke up still not knowing what to do on the big Millennium New Year's Eve, which is in two days. Yesterday Russell invited me to go with him and some friends to the Mall for the spectacular ceremony and fireworks display, and I said I would let him know. Even though this will be a once-in-a-lifetime experience and I love being part of historic public celebrations, I still hadn't talked to Terri about her plans, and I knew she wouldn't want to go to the Mall with Russell and his crazy friends. I hadn't heard from her in a few days and I was afraid to call her and learn that she had already made plans that did not include me.

Instead of calling Terri, I decided to go see her. I got dressed and went trucking over there, but when I got to her building I realized that I was about to kill any possibility of going to the Mall. Either Terri would invite me to spend New Year's Eve with her and I would have to sit around all evening listening to her moan about how lonely she is, or even worse, she would tell me that she already had New Year's Eve plans with some other woman and then I would be too depressed to go to the Mall with

Russell and his friends. So I just stood there frozen in front of Terri's building, and then it occurred to me that she could look out the window and see me, so I started walking around the block. I walked all the way around the block, feeling like some imbecile, and when I got back around to Terri's street I saw her up ahead, walking toward her building in her purple fleece jacket, carrying two shopping bags. She went into her building, and I said, "This is ridiculous," so I walked up toward her building, determined to ring her buzzer, and then my house mates Johnny and Guillermo appeared from around the corner. They yelled "Joanna!" as though they hadn't seen me in five years and they scurried up and started telling me about some drag queen getting thrown out of the Green Parrot and the police coming and I wasn't hearing a word of it. I just kept looking over at Terri's building, and then all of a sudden she walked out the door. She saw us and she called, "Knadel!" and instead of excusing myself and going up to her I just yelled lamely, "Hey, where ya going?" and she said she had to go to get her watch repaired and walked off toward Connecticut, leaving me there with Guillermo and Johnny and their silly story about the drag queen who was kicked out of the Green Parrot. After a few minutes, they went off to visit a friend and I walked home feeling very disconsolate about my aborted mission.

I am so indecisive lately. It's because I'm feeling insecure. Not only is the woman I love always just out of my reach, but I'm in this strange city where I don't know anyone, living in a house full of derelicts who fuck strange men they find on the street and steal other people's food

53

from the refrigerator and mince through the house with little pieces of Kleenex in their hair. I'm living a bizarre life, like some character in a Jim Jarmusch movie. At least I'm not one of those Y2K goofballs who are all over the TV news, crowding into supermarkets to stock up on water and canned goods in case everyone's computer goes kaplooey at midnight. I feel normal compared to them. Honestly, do they really think the banks and elevators and Wall Street and the supermarkets and the water and gas companies didn't hire enough geeks to prevent the civilized world from coming to an end?

Something just occurred to me. I'll bet Terri's shopping bags today were chock-full of canned food, water, and batteries! In fact, she was probably leading the frenzied pack down the aisles at the Safeway. She's always concerned about her safety and security. She told me that when we were kids during the Cold War and had to crouch under our desks for those inane security drills that I always thought were like a big game, she took it seriously and folded her arms over her head exactly like they told her to do. I'd better not call her any more today, or she'll start telling me how many cans of soup she bought, and how many cans of each *kind* of soup she bought, and I won't be able to resist making fun of her.

I'll wait until tomorrow to call her. If she had made any big plans for New Year's Eve, she probably would have called and told me.

I am lying on my bed in my tiny little room, watching the Millennium festivities on TV. Eleven glowing Ferris wheels are lined up along the Champs Elysées. It's amazing. I don't want to watch the festivities on the Mall because it will make me sad that I'm not there, so I'm watching ceremonies from other parts of the world.

I won't let myself think about Terri having dinner at a chic downtown place called Jaleo's with the publicity manager at the Bouncing Bear Theater, where she works during the evening. I'm sure that if I had called her early enough she would have made plans with me instead of some dumb woman she hardly even knows. But still it was a big bummer to hear that she's spending New Year's Eve with someone else. I asked her if the publicity manager is gay, and she said the woman *doesn't know yet*. What the hell is that supposed to mean?

I was so bummed out after I talked to Terri that I couldn't get it together to call Russell about the Mall excursion, and by the time I did call him, at 3 p.m. today, he had already left. His lover answered the phone and gave me a hard time: "*Child*, didn't he say to call him

by two? You *know* he was going early to get a good spot."
Oh, well, my bad. Did you ever hear that expression? "My
bad." I think it's one of the most annoying expressions of
all time. I'm using it to punish myself for having to sit in
this little tiny room all by myself on one of the most
momentous occasions of our era.

I hope Terri doesn't get the idea to help the publicity
manager figure out if she's gay. But I don't think she will.
She didn't use the word "date"; she just said she'd made
plans with this woman from the theater. I think if she
were planning to conclude the evening with a special
"nightcap" she would have used the word "date."

I suppose it was rude of me to call her at the last
minute and ask what she was doing. Oh! There are
Roman candles shooting up over Sydney Harbour! It's
really so beautiful. Even though I'm kind of lonely, I'm
glad that I'm here and not in that drippy little Cleveland.
And I have a bottle of pink champagne that I bought so I
can toast myself at midnight. I hope I can figure out how
to get the damned thing open. I hope the cork doesn't go
ricocheting off the wall and hit me on the head. That's
probably what will happen.

Terri is good at opening champagne. She's very compe-
tent with things having to do with the physical world.
Like programming digital devices and shit like that. Oh,
STOP IT! My bad. Oh, look. Wild dragons dancing on the
Great Wall of China. That is so awesome. I wish I were
there.

January 2000

The first day of the new Millennium started out nice. I woke up with the sun streaming in through my windows, wondering why I didn't feel like shit, and then I remembered that I couldn't get the champagne bottle open last night. I lay in bed, trying to decide what to do and then the phone rang and it was Terri, asking me if I would volunteer with her at the R Street mission, where they were having a holiday lunch for the homeless guys. My first thought was, "Harrumph. You take the publicity agent to Jaleo's and you want me to shlep with you to a mission." But I agreed to meet her. I always used to volunteer, before I turned into a self-obsessed lovesick blob. Even when I was a teenaged delinquent I volunteered at the Jewish Orthodox Home for the Aged and Head Start. (If you're Jewish, you can't be a pure juvenile delinquent. You always have to do something to water it down, like win a poetry contest or become a volunteer or help some teacher start a club for troubled students.)

I walked over to the mission at 14th and R, and some guys were outside, eating from paper plates. One of them called to me, "Come on in and have some lunch!

They got everything in there—ham, sweet potatoes, the works!" He made it sound as though I was about to enter Chez Paul. Terri, who is never even one minute late, was already in there, serving food behind a long table. They did have a nice spread, with baked ham and sweet potatoes and coleslaw and apple pie and layer cake. I stood next to Terri and started serving the food to a long line of men. We were joking around with them and the other volunteers, and I was having a pretty good time. But then I couldn't resist asking her how her New Year's Eve was and she said, "Wonderful!" I couldn't concentrate on putting food on plates and dealing with that at the same time, or else I would have demanded to know what was so wonderful about spending New Year's Eve with some sexually confused woman. But my generally free-floating anxiety hardened into a little red ball inside of me and I did my best to ignore it and kept slapping food on people's plates. And then I looked up and saw Jerome, Guillermo, and Johnny sitting at a table in the back, stuffing their faces full of food. They obviously had arrived and gotten served before I showed up.

I was mortified. Even if Terri hadn't been there, it would have bothered me to see my friends eating at a mission for homeless people. It gave me a kind of instant snapshot of my life, a middle-aged woman with normal ambitions living in a house with bums. And then I was ashamed for feeling embarrassed. I am a devout egalitarian. Every untouchable in India is my brother or sister. Why should I give a shit that my financially challenged buddies took advantage of some free food? But I was thinking, please don't come up here for seconds. I was so unnerved that I put a slice of cake on top of somebody's ham. Terri started laughing, then she looked at me and said, "What's the matter with you?" I said, "Nothing," but then I saw the boys striding up to us with big grins, and Guillermo was yelling, "Joanna Banana! Joanna Banana!" There was a fourth guy with them, who looked like a prison escapee. I pulled myself together and thought, Come on, Joanna, these are your buddies. So I introduced them to Terri, and Jerome gave me a suggestive look and said, "Oh, so this is Terri," and I jumped in brightly, "So what are you guys doing here?" and Jerome said, "We're having lunch. You should try the ham. It's as good as my aunt's." And Guillermo said, "She doesn't eat ham, you dummy. She's Jewish." I assured them that I did eat ham, but that I wasn't hungry. Terri said, "She eats like a bird," and the guys went back to their table to gorge on cake.

After they left, Terri said, "So why are your friends eating at a mission?" That's how she is. She doesn't have an ounce of tact. I said, "I don't know." And I really didn't. I didn't know if they were there because they were taking advantage of free food, or if they really didn't have enough money for groceries. I suppose it was a little bit of both. Terri said to me, "Doesn't Jerome work in a men's clothing store?" And I said, "No, that's Donald. Jerome is, uh, a sex worker." She got that expressionless look that I hate, and I was afraid she was going to ask me next what Johnny and Guillermo did for a living. "Oh, they go on burglary raids." But at least she spared me that. I wouldn't have told her that anyway. I would have said Johnny was a bartender and Guillermo worked at

Toys R Us, which is what they actually did do before they both got fired.

On our way out of the mission, Terri bumped into another volunteer, a woman she knew from her diversity training gigs, and she started gabbing with her. I didn't want to hang around waiting for her, so I said good-bye and left. And of course that nice mood I was in this morning when I woke up with the sun streaming through the windows is all shot to hell. I just can't seem to connect with Terri lately. Something always happens to screw it up. I know that if I had an ounce of self-confidence I would not be fazed by her going out with some drippy woman or seeing my house mates eating at a mission. I could handle it with my normal aplomb. But when I'm around Terri, I have no aplomb. That's the whole problem with my being in love. I just can't carry it off.

I called Terri today to see if she would exhibit an attitude after she learned that I lived with a bunch of street people, and my fears were realized when she used *that* voice with me. She has two voices, the super-interested one and the preoccupied one. She was using the preoccupied one. I could have told her that I was just diagnosed with terminal cancer and she would have used the same tone, asking me what treatment had been prescribed and how long I had to live. She just goes through the motions of the conversation. I timidly asked her if she wanted to go out for sushi with me tonight, and she said she had "plans." I said, "With whom? With that woman who doesn't know if she's a lesbian?"

"That's the one," Terri said.

"Are you going to try to help her with her little problem?" I asked.

"I don't know," Terri said.

"What do you mean, you don't know?" I said loudly. "She sounds like an idiot."

Terri got pissed. "She's not an idiot," she said. "You didn't come out until you were forty-five. Were you an idiot?"

"Yes, I was," I said. "I was a total idiot. I curse every goddam day I didn't come out. If this woman is hiding the fact that she's gay, she is an idiot. She's destroying her whole life so that people will like her."

"You don't know anything about her," Terri said. "You're just projecting."

"I am not," I said. I couldn't believe how infantile I was being.

Terri steered the conversation to a less volatile subject and started telling me about getting her furnace serviced and how the guy did something to it and then she had to have some other guy come and fix it, but her conversational maneuver had the effect of pissing me off more because it seemed as though she cared more about her stupid-ass furnace than she cared about me. When she noticed that I wasn't responding to anything she was saying, she stopped talking and we said goodbye to each other and hung up.

And now I've spent the past six hours since our conversation hating myself for losing my composure over the phone and obsessing over whether or not Terri will try to help what's-her-name decide whether or not she's gay. I'm lying in bed, twisting it around in my mind, over and over. If I *had* been diagnosed with terminal cancer, at least I wouldn't feel *stupid* about being so obsessed. For God's sake, doesn't Terri have a right to go out with someone other than myself? It's not as though she's even had sex with her. Maybe she never will. She doesn't fuck every damn woman she has dinner with. She went out with that one woman who, she said, had breath that smelled "vaguely radioactive" and she never fucked her.

I have to stop writing. I have to throw up. It's because of that leftover samosa I ate after I talked to Terri. I should never eat samosas when I'm upset, especially from greasy-spoon Pakistani carry-outs. Very smart, Joanna.

Terri called today and invited me to dinner, and I drove over there with my bottle of wine, all frisky and full of hope. It's been a week since that creepy phone conversation, and I figured she'd probably gotten bored with what's-her-name and had decided that being with me was a lot more fun. I wore my black jeans, a green silk shirt, and some short leather boots, and Terri answered the door in baggy jeans, an old tee shirt that said "Caribbean cool," and slippers. But she somewhat compensated for her attire by serving a fantastic meal of grilled salmon, mixed vegetables, and wild rice from scratch. She even made the dessert, two little coconut tarts, and she opened a nice bottle of French wine. She's a fabulous cook. During dinner, we steered clear of sensitive subjects and talked about Willi, our mutual friend from Cleveland who had introduced us to each other, and then Terri told me about her landscaping plans for her backyard.

After we polished off the wine, I thought it would be nice to cozy up on the couch, but instead Terri ushered me into her office and fired up her computer and started telling me about all the women she was meeting in this chat room called the "pink palace." At first, I thought, "Well, she must not be all that excited about the publicity agent if she's going online to meet women," but then she started showing me photographs of these women she was meeting and I started getting depressed. I tried to be polite about the photos and said, "Oh, she's cute" about the first one and "Pretty hot" about the second one, but when she showed me a third one of some redhead I snapped, "She is dreadful. I don't know how you can even look at her." The woman really wasn't that bad, but I was so furious that it just slipped out. Terri got rid of her, but then, not taking the hint that I wasn't exactly having the time of my life, she started telling me about this Montana housewife named "Darla" that she was having cyber sex with. For God's sake. But did I have the good sense to say, "You know what? I really don't want to do this." No! I just stood there and pretended to be interested. (When I went home, I called Karen in Cleveland and she said, "You should have just gone home at that point." Duh.)

It gets worse. Terri sat me down in her chair and logged onto this other chat room and instructed me to join the conversation. I hate chat rooms and had no interest in doing this, especially since I was with *her*, but I went along with it. I wrote in "Werm" as an alias, which is Tommy's nickname for me, and Terri said "Knadel, do you really want 'Werm' to be the name you use to meet girls?" I didn't want to use Knadel, so I settled for "Peeps," my younger sister's name for me. Terri told me how to jump into a conversation, and I inserted myself into some puerile conversation about toenail polish (they must all have been femmes), and I started getting bored, having nothing to say about toenail polish, but then Terri said, "If you want to talk to any of them individually, you can arrange a private conversation," so I selected a woman called BonBon, who was the only one of the group who said she didn't wear toenail polish, and asked her if she wanted to talk privately. She said okay, and we went into the private room and I tried to flirt with her, but my flirting went over like a lead balloon, and after about one minute she wrote, "Uh, Peeps? I'm really not into continuing this." And then she left. Fortunately, Terri was in the bathroom at that moment and was not a witness to my rejection by BonBon.

When I was getting ready to go home, I said to Terri, "So how is that—uh—*person* you were going out with?" Terri smirked and said, "If you're talking about Sandra, we're going to a movie on Sunday." I said, "Oh, how nice," and Terri said reassuringly, "I haven't slept with her yet." But then, when I tried to kiss her good-bye on the lips, she turned her lips away and gave me her cheek. Fuck her.

I was so distraught after I left that I started to walk home before remembering that I had taken my car. The evening started so nicely and ended up with a big thud. She hasn't slept with her "yet"? That's a big fat comfort. I love the bitch but I really have to start meeting other women. The message of this evening is clear, even to me.

Jerome lit a match under me today. I was lying in bed this afternoon, staring at the ceiling, and he strolled into my room, asking to borrow ten bucks and a winter scarf. (The sky dumped a couple feet of snow on the city over the weekend.) I told him to stay awhile and he lounged across my little bed with his big back against the wall and his big feet on the floor and I told him about my aggravating night with Terri, and he said, "I keep tellin' you, she's a player. It's time to toss this one out and shop for a fresh head of cabbage." I burst out laughing and said, "I wouldn't even know what to do with a fresh head of cabbage," and Jerome replied in his Barry White baritone, "I'll tell you what you do with it. You nibble it leaf by leaf until you get to the meat and then you plunge in for the kill."

After Jerome left with my scarf and 10 bucks (neither of which I will get back), I snatched the *Washington Blade* up off the floor and started looking through the personal ads. Lesbian personal ads infuriate me. I wish that just one of these bitches would run an ad that says, "Come with your drama," "Baggage welcome," and "Me:

a fucked-up neurotic mess. You: Not ready for relationship because you're still all hung-up on your last one." Instead they all say, "No drama," "No baggage," and that kind of stuff. It's okay for *them* to have baggage and drama, but you can't. Fortunately there were a few ads that sounded okay, and I answered them using the 900 number.

I don't know if I'm ready to go out with other women. I'll probably just end up being *friends* with them. It's typical of me, to end up as everyone's good buddy. That's even what Terri wants me to be. Fuck all that. I'm *sick and tired* of being everyone's buddy and having nobody to rock my boat at night. What do I look like, one of those Sesame Street fuzzballs? I have a libido too, for God's sake. Friends are not the staples of your life, like meat and potatoes and vegetables. They're more like cereal. If you try to subsist on Cheerios and Raisin Bran and Special K all day long, year after year, eventually you start to feel hollow and empty, and everyone keeps telling you how *lucky* you are to have all these different cereals, and how *good* you are at keeping yourself stocked in cereals, and one day you realize that you're completely malnourished while they're sitting around fat and happy from dining on prime rib every night or, as Jerome would have it, stuffed cabbage.

But it was my fault. I took the path of least resistance. I'm good with friendships. My favorite thing to do is get together with my friends and talk for hours. I always want to know what's going on with them and I'm a fantastic listener. On the other hand, I was never able to succeed at romance, for obvious reasons. I went on all these dates with men and I couldn't figure out why I never looked forward to them. I hated opening my closet and trying to decide what to wear. I didn't give a shit what I wore. I always wished I could just get into bed and forget the whole thing.

I'll never forget looking in my closet to decide what to wear for my first date with Terri. I could live in that moment forever.

I am utterly hopeless.

I made a date with a woman who ran one of the ads. We didn't talk long, but I liked her lush, gentle, African-American voice, and she liked that I was a writer and I liked that she was an advocate for troubled kids, and we arranged to meet at the Persian restaurant on 18th Street. The next evening, I walked over there at our agreed-upon time and found Dee Williams, the hostess of our potluck, sitting at a candle-lit table. This is an example of what gay women are always talking about. It's a small community. (Actually, they always say it's an "incestuous" community, but I haven't experienced that, as yet.)

I fucked up the whole date with Dee, who looked adorable in a tight floral skirt and silky blouse that showed off her small bust. Dinner wasn't so bad because Dee talked about herself, telling me that she grew up in DC and attended school in California and moved around a bit, and finally returned to DC, where she became a professional advocate for children who are "in the system." She's been single for a year, ever since her girlfriend left her for another woman. (Dee reported this with admirable restraint, although when I looked at her eyes they were two fresh wounds.) I liked everything about Dee and sat there feeling awful that I didn't want to jump her bones right there over the table. After dinner, we went to a bar called Larry's for a drink and I drank three rum and cokes and then the date really degenerated further because I started talking and couldn't stop. Specifically I couldn't stop talking about Terri. I went on about how she was my first love, and it was like a big explosion, and I moved here to be with her, and blah blah blah blah blah, and I even went into how divine it was to have SEX with her, and whereas Dee's story about *her* old girlfriend took about ten minutes, *my* story about *Terri*, who wasn't even an actual *girlfriend*, took about an hour. I would have kept going but Dee interrupted me finally and asked me if I was ready for a new relationship, and I looked her bravely in the eye and said, "Oh yes, oh yes, I'm definitely ready for a new relationship, I mean there's no way things can work out with Terri," but it was so obvious I was lying, it was pathetic.

I was too depressed to go home, so I announced that I needed a cigarette, and Dee needed one too after listening to my yammerings all night, so we went to the Seven-11 and bought a pack of Camel Lights and went back to Larry's and smoked a bunch of them and talked about whether flies sleep. After we left and parted ways, I was very drunk. The snow was melting and there was a warm breeze and I decided to find a place to hide my cigarettes, since I didn't want to smoke them. I wandered over to New Hampshire Avenue and found an apartment building with a bench outside of it and buried the cigarettes under the bench, thinking how cool it would be to take Dee there the next time we went out and retrieve the smokes like a magician. That's how looped I was, to think that Dee would be the least bit impressed with a woman in her 40s who digs up a pack of cigarettes she'd planted, not to mention the absurdity of thinking that she would even go out with me again in the first place.

After my evening with Dee, I didn't want to talk to anyone about it, my mom or my sisters or my friends in Cleveland or Jerome or anyone. I just lay on my bed and chastised myself for five days. And then, today, Terri called and it was like the re-opening of a theater that had gone dark. "Hello, Knadel?" *Voom!* Floodlights. She re-membered that Sunday is my birthday, and she invited me to go with her to brunch and a play. She also said she bought me a cell phone. That's my Terri; she's so stodgy and practical, she has to *tell* you what she's bought you for your birthday instead of having a normal sense of whimsy like other people and wrapping it up and giving it as a surprise. But the best part of our conversation wasn't about the cell phone, but when, after I asked her (against my better judgment) how Sandra was, she told me they were "just friends." To be suddenly relieved of all the graphic little images that had been plaguing me for weeks was the best birthday present I could ever have.

After I hung up with Terri, I started calling everyone I knew and telling them about my disastrous date with Dee and that Terri and the publicity agent are just friends and that she's taking me out on my birthday. Nobody sounded all that thrilled about it. My mom politely said, "That's very nice" and my sister said, "Oh, fuck her" and Tommy said I'm a sputnik and she's my earth and I will spend the rest of my life circling around her and when I told Jerome he said I blew it with Dee and I'm going to end up getting my female companionship in an old age home. But I don't care what they all say. Well, I do. But if they can't encourage me on my great quest for love, I'll just have to go it alone. The greatest heroes listen to no one. They forge ahead on their own, and public opinion be damned.

February 2000

My birthday was perfect. It was like a symphony by Mozart or Tchaikovsky, without the melodrama of Rachmaninoff or—who's that guy who wrote *The Rite of Spring?*—Stravinsky. It was Haydn, not Wagner. It was Brahms, not Beethoven during his hysterical deaf period. But maybe I'm getting a bit carried away, to compare my birthday to a great symphony. I suppose it was more like a movement, not a whole symphony. But a movement can be memorable, too.

Terri was all excited to give me my cell phone, which she had already programmed with her and my parents' numbers on speed dial. To tell the truth, I never really wanted a cell phone, figuring it would just complicate my life, but Terri insists that I need one because I drive all over the city for my job. Knowing me and my mouth, I'll probably become one of those obnoxious people who traipses around the street talking to people in a loud voice.

After Terri gave me the phone and a very funny card, we drove up to Silver Spring, MD (about 20 minutes away) and we met Tiny and Lou for brunch at the Indian

Gardens. They had a birthday balloon set up on my chair and gave me a homemade card with an elephant on it— Tiny remembered that I like elephants. The Indian meal was outstanding, which surprised me because it was a buffet and I usually hate buffets because the food gets cold and lumpy, but the buffet food at this place was hot and fresh and spectacular. The wait staff were attentive and filled our water glasses, and the nan was crusty and warm, and the company was delightful. It was nice to see Tiny again and I liked her girlfriend, Lou. We sat and laughed ourselves silly about Terri's father, who goes into excruciating detail about every moment of his life and doesn't ask Terri anything about herself, and Tiny's father, who eats mashed potatoes with his hands—he picks them up, makes little balls from them, and pops the balls in his mouth—because that's how he learned to eat them in Poland. Tiny has told him, "Dad, they do not eat mashed potatoes that way in Poland, I have Polish friends and none of them eat their potatoes that way," and he says that her friends don't come from some specific region in Poland where it's the custom to eat potatoes that way.

There was one briefly annoying moment, when, during a lull in the conversation, Tiny gave Terri a little smile and said, "Have you seen Sandra lately?" and Terri said yes, and then gave her a look like Let's not talk about this. Sandra is the publicity agent. I don't know why Tiny brought up this Sandra person since Terri isn't even dating her; they're just friends. Tiny can be annoying sometimes. She thinks I'm a crazy to be in love with Terri; the last time I saw her, when she came to Cleveland for Terri's mom's funeral and I had recently fallen in love with Terri and was totally hysterical, she said, "Protect your heart," and I thought it was the most idiotic thing I'd ever heard. Tiny was in love with Terri for three years and she said it was "three years of hell." At least I'm not in hell. Or if I am in hell I like it, so it's better than *her* hell, which to hear her tell it was exceedingly unpleasant. Anyway, she's not in hell anymore because now she's with Lou and they seem happy together.

After brunch, Terri took me to see *A Midsummer Night's Dream* at Montgomery College. It was a fine performance, with a lot of crazy improvisation, and I felt so contented sitting there next to Terri. I think she was contented too. Our arms were touching throughout the play and it was comfortable. The whole time I had not one moment of fear, not one moment of thinking, well, when is *this* all going to blow to smithereens? I think it was from watching all those idiotic fools in love, acting even more ridiculous than I, with their jackass heads.

After the play, we went back to Terri's and watched TV in her room. We lay on her bed and drank some wine and then I cuddled against her and she put her arm around me. We found an animated show called *South Park* and I wanted to change it, but Terri said, "No, no, Knadel. You'll love this." I couldn't believe this crazy cartoon. All these little characters were running amok, cursing one another out and dissing the principal of the school and making allusions to drugs. We were in hysterics over it. After the show, Terri turned off the TV and we lay there talking for a while. At one point Terri looked at me and said, "I wonder if you're going to start getting under my skin." And I said, "Count on it." I know she was drunk, but I think she meant it anyway.

That was yesterday, and I'm still high. She's going to be mine. I know it. Oh come on, Joanna, how many times have you thought that and then she slips away—usually that very same day? But how can she run away from such irresistible music? Right now, the violins are shrieking gratitude and the piano is bouncing along like a hobo with a full belly and the tuba is oom-pah-pah-ing and I'm the music pouring forth. Suddenly I know what Tommy means about classical music being superior to rock 'n' roll. Classical music doesn't just stay down here. It starts down here and then goes all the way up and out.

I suppose Tommy would say, "Werm, you know nothing about classical music." And he's right. I should stop writing and call some people on my cell phone. When it comes to talking on the phone, I'm a maestro.

Terri just called and asked me to meet her for dinner at Sushi Taro on 17th Street. I'm going to wear my black jeans and purple and red sweater. I wonder what she wants to tell me. She had this tone in her voice when she called—a slight formality that suggests this is not an idle invitation. I think she's going to tell me she wants to date me. Her father once said to her about me, "She seems like a nice girl; why don't you give her a tumble?" A tumble? I laughed when she told me that. But if she wants to "give me a tumble," I won't object.

Maybe she just wants to eat sushi. If that's the case, I need to make sure we don't sit at the sushi bar. If we do, Terri will spend the whole evening chattering with the sushi chefs and not pay attention to me. To keep her focused on me, I'll wear a pinch of musk oil. I'll put it behind my ears, and it will mix with the fake fur on the hood of my jacket and I'll be able to smell it for weeks. I love that!

I'm nervous. The walk will do me good. Forget driving. I'll never find parking. That's the one thing about this city that irritates me. You can't just go somewhere, like in New

York, where you automatically take public transportation. You have to plot it. "Do I walk? Do I drive? Do I take the bus or the train?" Often driving seems like the best option, but then you have to think, "Will I find parking?" And more often than not the answer is, "Not without a lot of aggravation." So then you might simply decide not to go, like if it's to buy a new watch-band. But when you have a date for dinner you can't just not go, so you have to figure out how to get there. The advantage to me of walking this evening is that my hair curls up nicely in the moist chilly air and I will enter the restaurant looking healthy and glowy rather than pinched and stressed the way I would after driving around and around competing with all those yoyos for a parking space. It's like a mad game of musical chairs out there. Musical Chairs with Cars. Sounds like the name of an album, don' it? (Want a Hertz Donut? —*Sure! Ouch!* Hurts, don' it? Ha ha ha ha ha . . .)

I'm lying here in this teeny tiny room in Washington, DC with no friends, where I'm a nobody. It's not funny. Stop laughing. Crying. Whatever it is I'm doing. I'm going to write because I can't just lie here like wet cement the way I've been doing for the past three days.

I don't understand it. I don't understand why she would want to date that publicity agent instead of me. She told me before that they were just friends. I suppose she just told me that so I wouldn't be upset and so she could give me my cell phone, which she probably bought months ago and she didn't want to be stuck with it. But Sandra didn't even know whether or not she was a lesbian. What did Terri do to her to make her realize what she was? I can't stand thinking about it. Thinking about it is worse than being eviscerated with a samurai sword. And I acted so wimpy when Terri told me at dinner that she and Sandra were dating each other and that she was scared to tell me but it would mean so much to her if she could have my support. And first I told her there was no way that I could be supportive, but she looked so crest-fallen that I drank as much sake as I could and started joking around with her, giving her the impression that I won't abandon her, but I will because I can't even speak to her as long as she's dating Sandra Finch.

I wonder how long this thing will last. I hope not more than two more weeks, but even if it's two weeks that will be two weeks of hell. Maybe she's already realized that this person is not The One. Oh god save me. If she wants a relationship so badly, why isn't she having one with *me*? I don't understand it. But why should I have just *assumed* that we were headed toward a relationship? When I think about it, we haven't done any girlfriend things since I moved here. We haven't made out, we haven't had sex, we haven't even kissed or *talked* to each other like girlfriends. We went to a movie and a Vietnamese restaurant and talked on the phone about where to get my car fixed and we went to brunch and a play. We lay on her bed a couple of times, but we didn't actually *do* anything on her bed. But still, she said I was getting under her skin. I know she loves me. I don't understand why she would want to be with *Sandra Finch* and not *me*. The woman is all fucked up. She has an eating disorder and was even hospitalized for it at some point in her life. Of course, I was hospitalized for being a pyromaniac, but that was a long time ago when I was just a teenager, and anyway, I'm not setting fires to trash bins anymore, but I'm sure Sandra Finch still has an eating disorder. She probably runs in the bathroom and throws up every time she's eating out with Terri, who takes her eating excursions very seriously and wants everyone with her to get as ecstatic about eating as she does.

But what if, in spite of all that, Terri falls in love with

her? What if they move in together and decide to have a commitment ceremony? And they invite me to it? Of course I wouldn't go. Oh shut up, Joanna. Just shut up. God, I'm so upset. I can't eat. I can't read or talk to anyone. I can't even watch TV. All I can do is lie here on this stupid bed and then shlep to work and then fall back on the bed. The only reason I'm not suicidal is that I'm too weak and indolent to kill myself. I couldn't just get up off my ass and *do* it. Not that I really want to. But if I had any guts I probably would. In high school, I was the only one in science class who couldn't prick her own finger with those little pins the teacher handed out so we could determine our blood type. Someone had to do it for me. I act like I'm such tough stuff, but really I'm a feeble-hearted little wimp.

I'm so lonely. I have always had plenty of friends, but I've been so obsessed with Terri that I haven't even made any real friends here, except for these unstable men in my house. It's not the same as having close friends and family members around, caring about everything that happens to you, like I do in Cleveland. Not that I would ever move back to that dump. But that's what's so scary. I have nowhere to go. What will I do? Move back to New York in the middle of having a nervous breakdown? That's a joke.

Oh, god. That's what I'm having. A nervous breakdown. I'd better get up off of this bed and *do* something. I'll go out and have a few drinks. I need to get some perspective. It's not the end of the world. Well it is, but the world can be saved. All that has to happen is for Terri to break up with Sandra Finch. She's not going to

87

keep seeing Sandra Finch when the world is at stake. She will consider it her *responsibility* to break up with Sandra Finch. She has an unerring sense of responsibility.

I'm going insane. I have to get out of this room.

March 2000

I am drunk and seized by clarity! What I realize all of a sudden is that there is really nothing to be upset about! Stop with the exclamation points already! Whoops! I dropped my notepad and picked it back up.

Shit. I really am fucking smashed. But the thing that I realized, and I'm sure it's not just because I'm drunk, is this: *I am actually a very fortunate person!* When I compare myself to the rest of the world, I don't have it so bad at all. Here I was, completely devastated because the girl I want is *attracted* to someone, and then I thought of how much worse off so many other people are. Like all the thousands of people who have been married for *decades* and have houses and kids and their whole lives invested in these relationships and then all of a sudden their husbands and wives declare they don't love them anymore and walk off with the . . . the . . . the *secretary*. Or the guy they met at the wine and cheese store. Talk about *devastating*. And *then* the cheaters have the nerve to want the *kids*, or at least visitation rights, and can you imagine how awful it would be to have to gussy up your kids and shuttle them off to the person who took your husband or wife away, leaving you in abject agony, despair, and humiliation for months, years, and possibly *forever*? And knowing your ex is going to try to get the kids to call that person *Mom* or *Daddy*, and even though you want your kids to *hate* this person and to hate your ex even more you have to put on a phony little act on visiting days, smiling and zipping their jackets and saying, "Now tell Daddy not to forget to send back your juicy-juice this time!" or "Have a wonderful time camping with shithead and Medusa, darlings!" and maybe you even have to *drive* them to shithead's new house (which is probably bigger and nicer than yours) and you have to drop them off right in front or even take them to the door and have shithead open the door with a big happy smile, and you would like nothing better than to drive a knife through that black, cheating heart but you can't because your children are standing right there.

And imagine going through all that squabbling over the house and money and possessions with the divorce lawyer, and knowing your friends, or at least some of them, still *like* shithead and even get together with the shiny new couple to play cards and drink and laugh (at you), and you know that when they all talk about the breakup some of them are saying that you weren't exciting or smart or evolved enough to keep shithead's interest, when the reality was that you were working your *tuchas* off so that shithead could take more and more classes and obtain advanced degrees, which he or she used to obtain a more prestigious job which helped to attract whore or scumbag.

So now I don't feel so lonely, realizing that *everybody* is living in hell. Or, at least, millions of other people. And most of them are worse off than I am. It's like we're living in a giant Auschwitz with these agonized, tortured, humiliated people stumbling around like the walking dead, wondering how they're going to get through the next day.

Maybe it's not nice to compare regular life with Auschwitz. I take it back. But still, it would be better to be a dog than a human, when you really think about it.

I'm going out to drink more. This is great. I'm coming up with all these insights. Next I'm going to figure out how to kill Sandra.

I can't believe this. I'm in *jail*.

I know it was my fault, but I had such a whopping hang-over this afternoon and this cop just picked the wrong time to mess with me. I wasn't bothering anyone—I was just sitting on the sidewalk, leaning against the DC government building on 14th Street, eating a turkey Subway sandwich, and all of a sudden this bulldyke-looking cop strutted up to me and barked at me, "MA'AM, YOU CAN'T DO THAT; LET'S MOVE IT!" Her choice of address upset me first of all. I felt so humiliated, to be called ma'am while being reprimanded for sitting on the sidewalk; it made me feel like a crazy old street woman instead of like a defiant young rebel, which I would have felt like if she had called me "miss" or "young lady" or something of that nature—not that I'm young enough anymore to be called those things. I was nauseated from all the rum and cokes I drank yesterday and was in a horrible state, and I was crying over Terri and trying to eat this sandwich with tears running down my face, and this cop just couldn't just see I was upset and leave me alone, because God forbid some tour bus should cruise by with the guide boasting about the spanking "New U Street" and the tourists should

94

catch wind of some deranged woman sprawled on the side-walk. So she said "Ma'am, you can't do that, let's move it!" and I told her . . . well, I told her to get the fuck out of my face.

Obviously, I over-reacted. But when you're in emotional anguish and someone struts up to you and barks at you like a dog, you don't necessarily react rationally. Even if it's a cop. Of course, Dottie (that was her name) didn't take too kindly to my telling her to get the fuck out of my face, and she pulled me up by my arm and my sandwich fell on the side-walk in a glop, and I screamed and yanked my arm away while she tried to pull me up and then a blond white cop trotted up out of nowhere and said, "Dottie, you need some help?", and Dottie said, "Got a Section 8 here, Dave," refer-ring to the Army's designation for nutcase discharges, which I found quite insulting. Then Dave and Dottie pulled me up and cuffed me behind my back, and they stuffed me into a patrol car and took me to the 3rd District police station, and here I am in this cell. What makes this whole thing especially pathetic is that I had no one to call for my One Phone Call, so I can't even get out.

I've been in here for five hours and it's a real drag. One, it's humiliating; two, I need a shower and a change of under-wear; and three, I'm wondering how much this little adven-ture is going to cost me.

Actually I'm not humiliated to be in jail; I'm humiliated to think about Dottie yanking me off the sidewalk and my sandwich splattering all over and I'm humiliated because I smell. If I could just punch Dottie in the face, have a shower, and be assured that I wasn't going to have to pay some whopping fine, I would be perfectly contented to sit

here. I've never minded being in jail all that much, probably
because I associate it with my good times being locked in
the bin when I was fourteen. When you're emotionally distraught, it can be a relief to get locked up and treated like a
child, even if the "parents" are mean and won't let you out
of your room. And this time it's going to be far less of a
hassle than the last time I got popped, about ten years ago,
for a DWI, which in our society is considered worse than
murder. Even though this time I resisted a police officer,
they're probably not going to toss some white woman
going through an emotional crisis into the DC jail with all
those street women.

Where's my captain friend? The captain is my buddy.
He came by my cell a couple hours ago and asked if I
needed anything, and I said I would really like some paper
and a pen because I'm a writer and would like to write
something, and he gave me some paper and a little nub
pencil without any point, God forbid I should stab myself.

But now I'm done writing and I need some food. I'm
going to demand another turkey sandwich from Subway.
They owe it to me because the bulldyke made me drop the
one I bought this afternoon. And I would like a lemonade
to go with it, but they'll probably bring milk. They always
do. It's their way of being mean to you for being a bad girl.
No LEMONADE FOR YOU TODAY, MISSY! DRINK YOUR
MILK!

God, I can't believe this is happening. I'm really too old
to be thrown in jail for misbehavior. I know I'm getting off
on it a little, which is even more disturbing. Maybe I'll tell
them I need a shrink to determine why I get a sexual
charge from being in jail. No, forget that. What I need is

just to chill out a little. Jail is probably the perfect place for me right now. If only I could have a shower and a change of clothes. They could give me one of those jumpsuits. Before I put it on maybe they could get Dottie to . . . oh, never mind. That's too sick. That is just too sick.

I'm back home, whoop-di-doo! Now I'm a certified DC jailbird. The only problem is, I can't really brag about it because if I tell people how I landed in jail it would sound so lame:

I was sitting on the sidewalk, eating a sandwich.

You were what? Well, why the fuck didn't ya get up, peabrain?

But maybe I can redeem myself by reporting that I did have a fistfight in jail. Every red-blooded American girl should have at least one fistfight on her dossier. At least, that's what I tell myself to keep from feeling ridiculous.

I didn't mind being in jail, but it became progressively more aggravating. For dinner, they brought me the most horrible meal possible—a baloney sandwich on stale bread and milk. They didn't even give me any mustard. I looked at the little box that the crewcutted white cop had slid through the bars and yelled ICH!," and then I said, "I can't eat this. Take it back and get me a quarter pounder with cheese!" Now of course I knew he wasn't going to actually do that, I was just making a little joke, but he didn't pick up on my humor. He turned to another cop who was standing there and laughed at me snidely, saying, "She wants us to get her a quarter pounder with cheese," and the other cop said something low so I couldn't hear him even though they were standing right there, and they both snorted like I was some kind of honky prima donna who was demanding special treatment. I felt so bad when the cops didn't just humor me, like "Oh sure and how about a nice soft pillow for your bed?"—that instead they sneered at me, they took me the whole wrong way. I couldn't eat the sandwich, so I went to sleep hungry on that awful bed-slab they have in jails, with my body all funky and smelly since they didn't have a shower in the holding cell area.

The next morning at 7 a.m. they hauled me out of the cell and took me downtown (I'm surprised they processed me that fast—I think they really wanted to get rid of me) to the local courthouse on Indiana Avenue, and they tossed me in a holding cell with about eight other women. They were all hookers and drug addicts except two young women who had been busted putting up signs for the protest against World Bank and the International Monetary Fund, who are charging underdeveloped countries exorbitant interest on debts. When they put me in the cell, the other prisoners paid no attention to me because they were having a discussion. The two activists were trying to explain to the street chicks the importance of their protests, and the street chicks were looking at them as though they were kangaroos. A skinny, young hooker said, "Well I wouldn't know about that," and looked away into space, trying to make them disappear, and then a busty hooker in a yellow tank top said ,"Why should I care what happens in Kenya? Them niggers down there don't care what happens to *me*." And *then* the thing happened that started it off. A slightly older woman, a skinny redhead with big tits and yellow lipstick, clomped up to the second woman and hit her on the shoulder. She said, "Peaches, don't talk to them! Don't talk to them slimy-ass bitches! What's wrong with you?" Then she walked away, saying, "Ugly cunt motherfuckers." The two young women just froze. I was really pissed off because I respect them—they are so stout-hearted and sincere and *right* about everything—the whole country's going to the dogs morally, with six corporations running everything, and nobody gives a fuck about anyone else, and money has finally, officially become God. These kids know that corporations are just too big, they have too much power and the people in them act like they're stupid, "the computer won't let me do this, the computer won't let me do that, the system is down, so go fuck yourself"—and if they treat middle-class Americans like that, imagine how they bully and browbeat the people from underdeveloped countries. So here are these kids who are arrested for rebelling against the amorality that has overtaken us and some nasty bitch calls them "ugly cunt motherfuckers." I said "What's the matter with you, woman—why are you calling these people ugly cunt motherfuckers? They're trying to do some good in the world and there's no reason for you to diss them like that. That's just *wrong*." The redhead flung her head around to look at me, really seeing me for the first time, and she leaned over toward me, stabbed her finger at me, and said, "I was not addressing you, white scum." I glared at her and she said, "DO YOU HEAR ME? I SAID I WAS NOT ADDRESSING YOU, WHITE SCUM," and she came up to me and pushed me, hard. And I *slugged* her! Right in the side of her face. She grabbed a clump of my hair and wouldn't let go, and we fell to the floor, and I started pounding at her face, trying to get her to let go of my hair, and everyone was yelling and screaming. In about thirty seconds, three cops came in and pulled us apart, and damned if that redhead ended up with my hair in her fist as a trophy. They shuttled me out of there and took me right into the courtroom and one of them talked to the bailiff, who interrupted the judge and said something to her. The judge then disposed of the young fellow standing before her, and then called me over, before I even had to sit down.

The judge, an imposing brown woman with salt-and-pepper hair named Louise Holmes, looked at me and asked, "What in God's name is going on with you?" And I told her. I told her what happened, how I was eating my Subway sandwich and the cop pulled me and I was already extremely upset and I just lost control. Then I told her the woman I'm in love with is with someone else, and I'm out of my mind over it, and I moved here because of her, and I started to cry. Judge Holmes' eyes softened. Then she said in her deep voice, "Now you listen to me. You need to forget about this person who clearly does not love you. You cannot just keep beating a dead horse. Look at me!" I did, and she repeated what she'd said. "You need to move on with your life. And that's just what you are going to do. If you continue to engage in the kind of behavior that brought you in here, defying police officers and lying around in the street like a derelict, I dread to think where you'll end up. Are you listening?" I said yes, and she said she was going to sentence me to three days in jail but would suspend the sentence. Then she said, "I am doing this with the stipulation that you pull yourself out of this rut you're in. You need to start meeting people who can help you forget about this woman who *clearly does not want you.*" I wished she would stop saying that, but I wasn't going to tell her. But then she completely astonished me. She said, "Have you heard about the monthly potlucks for lesbians here in DC?" I stared at her, thinking, now how the hell does *she* know about the lesbo potlucks? Then she asked the bailiff for a pen and piece of paper and she dashed off a phone number—from *memory*—and handed it to me. "Here," she said. "Here's the number of the woman hosting the next event." I looked at the paper and it said, "Cherry Hill," with the number written beneath it. I was rather intrigued that this judge Holmes knows a dyke named Cherry Hill so well that she had memorized her phone number. I'm still intrigued, and I intend to call this Cherry Hill tomorrow. I had a good time at the last potluck at Dee's house, and I need to get back to having a social life.

I have to admit that I feel a little guilty about my encounter with the DC law. I know that, after all is said and done, the cops did give me special treatment, in spite of not bringing me my quarter pounder with cheese. They got me in and out of jail real fast. Even the judge took me before all those black people that were sitting there on those benches. I'll bet my redheaded nemesis will be in the clink for the next six months. No wonder the black folks in this town have such an attitude.

Terri will never, ever know any of this. Fuck her anyway. I wish that judge had sent me away somewhere. I'm very tired.

April 2000

Considering what a mess I am, I would consider the potluck a success. I called Cherry Hill the day after court, as per instructed by the good judge, and she answered the phone and spoke to me in a loud, nasal, suburban, Jewish voice. I know that sounds awful, but how else am I going to describe it? She yelled (in her normal voice) that her women's potlucks were open to all lesbians, and she *commanded* me to come to the next potluck on Saturday afternoon. So on Saturday I went to the supermarket and bought some potato salad (I'm so inspired) and then I drove up to Cherry Hill's gorgeous stone house in Kalorama, one of the richest neighborhoods in DC.

Cherry Hill was a short, voluptuous woman with a trumpeting laugh to match her stentorian voice. She began spiriting me around her beautiful house with its stone floors and skylights and stunning rugs and paintings, introducing me to women gabbing over paper plates full of food. In one of three living rooms, I found my drinking buddies from the last potluck, Bette, Jean, and Pia. Bette enfolded me in a busty hug. I was disappointed not to see Dee, but a tall, coltish-looking woman was sitting with them, and she had a nice, casual-butchy look, with her jeans and seersucker shirt and blond, surfer-boy hair.

Cherry went to answer the door and Bette cattily said, "Leave it to a lesbian to entertain with paper plates even though she's a millionaire. You know, this would never happen at a gay boys' party." And I replied, "Well, gay boys wouldn't even *have* a potluck." For some reason it didn't bother me to be all snide and teenager-ish with Bette. Maybe it's because she's not shallow. During the last potluck at Dee's, she shared fascinating chunks of information about everything from Georgetown etiquette to Scandinavian literature to the brain's limbic system. Not only is she well-read and intellectually curious, but underneath the cattiness is a whole lot of kindness.

I told the girls my whole jail adventure and they whooped and hollered. I was a little sheepish about revealing my lunacy to the new girl, Kimba Patterson, but she didn't seem to mind at all. In fact, she seemed to take a particular interest in me and I really took to her. She was understated, with a soft voice, but I could tell that she wasn't shy because her green eyes had a mischievous sparkle, the corners of her mouth kept flickering as though she wanted to laugh, and she had a casual way of speaking, not nervous at all. She told us she saw a rainbow the day before, and I teasingly scoffed at this, saying I'd never even seen a rainbow, and she said she saw them all the time. She mentioned that she had a twin sister who lived in Florida, and that she grew up in a small town outside of Kent, Ohio, and when I said I was from Cleveland her eyes lit up. She confided in me that she doesn't like DC, with its stiffness and workaholism. She has two master's degrees and a high-level job at NASA, but she's still a down-home country girl at heart. I said I hoped she didn't go back to Ohio anytime soon, and she said she didn't plan on it, and she invited me to an Orioles–Indians game at Camden Yard.

While I was talking to Kimba, Cherry Hill breezed up behind me and said, "Where did you get that sexy shirt?" I told her I got it at Chico's, and she gave me a big smile and said, "You should always shop at Chico's." Then Kimba left to go country-western dancing, and I went to the food table, and before I had a chance to rejoin my friends Cherry got hold of me and started interviewing me. She asked me if Kane was a Jewish name, and I said in my case it was, and she got a gleam in her eye and I thought, "Uh, oh." I said her name reminded me of one of my favorite songs, "Cherry Hill Park," and she said she kept her ex-husband's name rather than going back to being Cheryl Lipschutz. She asked me if I belong to the Jewish gay congregation that meets at the Jewish Community Center, and I said I did not because I was raised by socialist heathens and I'm a socialist heathen myself, and she said that was fantastic and that when she was growing up there were socialists living right next door. I asked her what she did for a living and she said she got "some money" from her divorce, so she doesn't have to work; she just has potlucks and serves on com-mittees, which means for a hyper-extrovert like her that she hobnobs around town schmoozing with everyone and probably not getting anything done. (I wanted to ask

109

her how she knew Judge Holmes but didn't want to bring up how *I* knew Judge Holmes, so I let it go for the time being.) Then, wasting no time, Cherry asked me if I wanted to meet her at Rosemary Thyme on 18th Street for lunch, say, on Wednesday. And I said yes.

I don't know exactly why I made a date with Cherry Hill. She has that foghorn voice and we don't seem to have much in common. But I need any distraction I can find from the ache that I get up with and go to bed with and walk with all day because I miss that stupid whore Terri. I know I shouldn't call her a stupid whore. It's not nice. Maybe that's why she doesn't want me. Because I call her a stupid whore. Actually she likes when I call her "whore." She laughs. But she wouldn't want me to call her stupid. She would say it simply wasn't true. "But I'm not stupid," she would say. Like I meant it literally. She's so *literal* about everything.

All things considered, I'm glad I went to the potluck and that I'm going out with Cherry Hill. I had a more rip-roarin' good time at Dee's potluck. But I was young and innocent back then, and now I'm a tarnished, broken-hearted jailbird, and I need to take whatever scraps of pleasure are offered me.

My date with Cherry Hill turned out to be very good. It was very, very good. If you catch my drift. Picture me standing here with a Mick Jagger leer (which should not be difficult because I still look a little bit like Mick). Not that I would presume to be as sexy as he is, but we all have our little moments, and yesterday was one of mine. So why do I feel so deflated about the whole thing today?

It all started because I couldn't wait to get out of the restaurant with her. As soon as we sat down, she started to embarrass me. She kept asking mundane questions, like, how old was I when I came out and what kind of woman is my type, and every time I answered she erupted with her trumpeting laugh. I was just answering honestly, but for some reason she found everything I said deliciously funny. Finally I told my jail story, which elicited a resounding screech that put all the others to shame. She did solve the mystery of Judge Holmes; she and "Louise," as she calls her, had never been intimate, they just served on a committee together. Upon hearing that disappointing news, I suggested that we walk over to my place since I had a couple hours to kill before work. (The whole time we were eating, I had been concentrating on her plump breasts to avoid looking at the other diners.)

We walked over to my house and went upstairs to my little room, which she thought was the most adorable thing she'd ever seen and said she wished she lived there instead of in her 18-room mansion because she is sick of all the upkeep. I decided to shut her up before the conversation got any more ludicrous, so I closed the door and we proceeded to have wild sex. I have a package of latex gloves that I bought to play sex games with Terri, and I haven't had that opportunity, but I put those gloves to good use with Cherry Hill. I pretended to be the nursing supervisor on a psychiatric unit and I ordered her to undress completely and lie on the bed. She asked me what she did and I said, "You know *exactly* what you did, Miss. You have been running through the ward like a crazy girl, and are upsetting the other patients. We're going to help you regain control over yourself." She kept protesting, saying, "No, no, please, I'll be good," and I said, "You have had plenty of opportunities to be good. Now just do as I say," so she took off her clothes and lay on my bed and I donned the gloves and said, "Spread your legs," and she did, and I inserted a finger into her and said, "This will relax you," and she started to laugh and I informed her that she would not be able to return to the unit until she cooperated. Of course, this made her laugh even harder—between gasps, because I was fucking her really good with practically my whole hand—and I told her the longer she kept that up, the longer she would have to submit to the treatment. Finally I withdrew my fingers and said, "It appears that you require more intensive treatment today." I stripped off my clothes and ordered her under the covers and got under there with her. I said, "As soon as you stop fighting me this will all be over." I put my leg between hers and re-inserted my fingers and fucked her harder than ever and she literally started screaming—it was a good thing everyone on my floor was out because they would have thought I was killing her. When she got that otherworldly look, I said, "All right, relax," and she came like Mt. St. Helens and I came too, just from sheer excitement.

It was the best sex I ever had, including with Terri. I was so relieved to finally bust loose that I told everyone I knew. Jerome was ecstatic and said Cherry should be my woman. My friends in Cleveland were shouting "Hurrah!" because I hadn't done the wild thing in such a long time. Even my mom voiced her quiet approval. She said, "That's very nice." (No, I did not give her the colorful details.)

The only problem with my tryst with Cherry is that it was a fleeting pleasure, like doing a snootful of cocaine. The woman is so annoying that I don't really want to see her again. She sounds like a high school orchestra tuning up every time she opens her mouth. She already called today to ask me what I was doing tomorrow evening, and thank god I could tell her I'm going to the ball game with Kimba. But she'll probably call me again and I'll have to tell her it was a one-shot deal. I did that a million times with men, having sex with them one time to prove something to myself and then running away from them. It's just such a crappy thing to do. If I had sex with these people because of uncontrollable passion, that would be one thing. But it's all about my ego, not my libido—I'm trying to prove my womanhood. And it ends up having the opposite effect. I end up feeling less of a woman than ever.

Kimba and I went to see the Indians play the Orioles at Camden Yards. Kimba is so much fun. I hope she didn't find me boring. I'm sure she did. She was so lively and charming and I was—I was *trying*. That's about all I could say for myself.

Kimba is a more suitable partner for me than Cherry Hill, but she's in love with a heart-breaker of a girl who is more of a female Lothario than Terri. Kimba had been with a fine woman for eight years, but the relationship lacked passion, and then Kimba got breast cancer, went through the whole mastectomy-chemo-hair-falling-out ordeal, and decided she wanted to live her life to the fullest, so she left her partner and ran off with this seductress, who was as elusive as her partner was loyal. They broke up a couple months ago, but in typical lesbian fashion they are still "friends," and Kimba still loves her and is furious with her at the same time.

Kimba told me all of this between bites of hotdogs (she wanted to get nachos, but I upbraided her and explained that you MUST eat hotdogs at a ballpark and she indulged me) and between good plays, during which

Kimba leapt up and screamed her head off. Kimba is a sports nut and her energy was infectious. It was a good game, with the Tribe winning on a two-run double by Jim Thome in the ninth. Kimba is also hilariously funny. When a guy a couple rows down got drunk and kept yelling stupid things at the players, she yelled, "Hey, shut up down there," and then she crunched up her hotdog wrapper and threw it and it hit him on the head. He didn't notice, but I just about died with laughter. Here's this competent professional woman who has risen through the ranks of NASA, but inside she's still this wild hillbilly girl. She's got a flow about her; she's not herky-jerky, like I am. She's very funny, tossing off these piquant remarks that made me laugh until I almost fell off the chair. She has an adorable, flashing smile and almond-shaped green eyes and a body that's nice to look at, coltish and leggy with a nice tight ass where the saddle would be. (She would say something real smart-ass in response to that.)

I felt kind of like a dud with Kimba. I was missing Terri during the whole game, which was ridiculous because I was with a woman who is my kind of people—funny, irreverent, and smart. And she's crazy about baseball, which means something to me because I'm one of those people who got taken to ball games by their dads as youngsters and who swell with bone-deep pleasure upon finding a ballgame while station-surfing; hearing "foul ball off the catcher's glove" over the low roar of a crowd is as soothing as the smell of a baby brother's sweat. Terri doesn't even like baseball. To her, a slider is probably some sort of treated dildo. I tried to have fun with Kimba. She made me laugh and I liked her so much, but I couldn't shake off that blunted feeling. Why can't I stop missing Terri? It doesn't go away. I still feel as though someone cut me open and scooped out all my insides.

I have a funny feeling I've reached the end of the road. I feel like doing something bad like smoking marijuana in front of the police station so I can see Judge Holmes again. Maybe she'll send me to some minimum security prison. I would like not having to make any decisions, not to mention being with all those bad girls. The problem is, there would be people in there trying to tell me what to do. I don't like people telling me what to do, unless it's someone of my choosing, like Judge Holmes. But if Judge Holmes ordered me into some prison to get told what to do by *other* people, that would be a Catch-22. It's like the old sally of my dad's: "You remind me of that man." "What man?" "The man with the power." "What power?" "The power of voodoo." "Who do?" "You do." "I do what." "You remind me of that man . . ."

I feel sorry for Dad. He so wanted to pull out all stops for my wedding. And here I am, gay. But I think he was relieved when I came out. Everything kind of fell into place at that moment. He said, "All that's important to me is that you be happy." And he meant it. He can be a monster sometimes, but I'll always love him for that.

May 2000

I have come up with a strategy for not feeling like a little nobody surrounded by world-beating honchos. I decided to write an article for the *City Rag*, DC's largest weekly (formerly known as "alternative") newspaper. I e-mailed a few story ideas to the editor, along with my credentials, and he sent me back an assignment. I put my top choice at the bottom, knowing that editors never choose stories at the top of your list, and that's the one he picked. I'm going to write about the gentrification of the U Street Corridor, which is my neighborhood, and how the old-time residents feel about it. It won't be a cover story, first of all because I'm a new writer for the paper and second, because the topic isn't suitable for a feature story; it's more newsy. He's going to use it for the Street Talk section.

I want to write this article because I've been upset by the racial tension in DC ever since I've moved here. My jail altercation with that hellcat who referred to me as "white scum" was just one indication. It seems to me that DC's black residents are so angry at being ignored and disregarded that they are mean. When you walk down the street, the black folks either pointedly ignore you or glare at you, and when you're in stores or other places they won't look at you even when they're waiting on you, and if you ask them if they have a certain item they automatically say "No," or "I don't think so," as though they want you to be disappointed and get a taste of how *they* feel as unempowered residents of a federal city that ignores them. The resentment is fueled by the fact that there aren't any working-class white people in DC for black folks to relate to. The only white people they ever see are power players in their expensive suits, tourists tripping around with their little maps, privileged college students, and older people shlepping around in boring clothes, who don't care how they look because they are rich.

In neighborhoods like mine, where whites are moving in, buying up property, and driving up housing costs, you can cut the tension with a knife. Middle-class flight and the 1968 riots destroyed the once-vibrant neighborhood, and now white urban pioneers are "bringing it back," pissing off the established residents. As is typical, many of the homesteaders are gay men. It's nice to see so many gay people around here, but it pains me that our black neighbors view us as invaders instead of allies. I want to go up to one of these black women who glare at me at the bus stop and say, "Listen woman, they did me wrong too! I've been disenfranchised just as you have!" But she would be likely to say, "That's your punishment for goin' against the Lord. So don't be cryin' to me, sinner!" And then she'd get up on the bus with her big behind glaring at me, leaving me feeling worse than I did before.

But this article cannot be personal. It will be straight journalism. I have no idea how it's going to come together, but it will get attention, because it's a hot subject in this town. Of course, I shouldn't be presumptuous, because the same thing could happen as what happened with my Coming Out piece that I wrote for the *Cleveland Free Times,* which I thought was going to be such a big sensation and there wasn't even one letter to the editor, and in my self-righteous irritation I refused to acknowledge that it was a terrible piece, with my dumb metaphor of wandering through the woods for thirty years. The problem was that I was all hung up on the impression I would make while I was writing it. With writing, the process is everything. You can't be preoccupied with the results—with all the respect you'll get from people and all the power you'll have over them and how you'll become rich and famous and win the girl and live happily ever after. You just can't do that. So stop doing it. Yes, you. Stop it. Right now.

June 2000

My story ran in last week's edition of the *City Rag*, and I did a good job. That's what the editor said after I sent it. "Good job." In editor's language, that means: "This is an absolutely perfect, fantastic piece."

I covered a lot of ground in just 1,500 words. What surprised me most was how many of the black folks I interviewed expressed the conspiracy theory that the powers-that-be are working together to force all the black people out of DC. Young man in Ben's Chili Bowl: "They got a plan. Take my word for it. They got a plan." One woman, a community organizer and editor of the newsletter *What's Goin' On*, described the psychological effects of gentrification: "A lot of our residents have been living in the same houses for their whole lives, had life-long relationships with their neighbors, and suddenly there they are, on blocks full of showpiece homes, half their neighbors gone, and their homes are the rattiest ones on the block. How would you feel if that happened to you?" There was a lot of trash-talking. Two young female cashiers: "These white ladies want us to stop what we doin' to help them. They say, Do you have this? Do you have that?" Cashier 2: "Get it yourself, bitch. 'Scuse me."

I included statements from one white guy who has been living in the neighborhood for less than a year. "The racial tension around here makes me uncomfortable. I come from New York City, where people of different colors interact and don't even think about it. Here, like, if you just nudge someone by mistake, it's gonna cause a major war. I accidentally bumped into this woman on the Metro escalator the other day and she was ready to rip me a new asshole. Pardon my French, but my language is squeaky clean compared to hers. Motherfucker this and motherfucker that, and these motherfuckers think they can come in here and do this and that . . . It wasn't pretty."

My writing was clear and succinct, my quotes were strong, and the organization was impeccable. Marty Engle was right; I did a good job. What gave me a special kick was that all my buddies in the house read it and they're all proud of me. Johnny and Guillermo came running into my room with a copy of the paper, gloating, and when their thug friends came galloping up the steps they thrust my article in their faces, saying, "Look what our woman Joanna wrote." I stopped into Jerome's room to return his air freshener and he said, "You did a fine job," just like the editor said. (The difference is, I'm sure the editor actually *read* the piece, but it was nice of Jerome to give me a little "attagirl.")

Kimba, who never gushes, told me she thought I did a good job on the story, and Bette, who does gush, called and said she brought the article to work (she designs computer adult education programs) and her colleagues said it was brilliant. To celebrate, the three of us went to this lesbo party with this horrid D.J. named Popo who plays house music, and Jean and Pia were in there and they had both seen my article and congratulated me. The five of us got drunk and crazy, and we accosted the D.J. with some song requests and she complied and let loose with some Carlos Santana (me) and Cher (Bette) and Dixie Chicks (Kimba) and some other rockin' stuff and we all danced up a storm. We decided to name ourselves "the Ditches"—short for Dykes in the House or something like that—I don't remember exactly because we were so drunk when we thought of it. But it has a nice ring. So now we have a gang. I love being in a gang because I'm very tribal, having grown up in a large family. (Kimba is the same way.)

The one thing that bothers me is that Terri still hasn't called. Maybe she still hasn't seen my piece. But how could she not have seen it? She sees everything. What if she saw it and hated it? Or what if she *never* sees it? She could be on one of her vacations. What if she's on vacation with . . . with *her*? Maybe she was just away for a long weekend when the paper came out, like for one of her diversity training jobs. But then when she came back I would think that one of her friends would have shown her the article. But maybe they wouldn't because they're so absorbed in their own lives that they would forget. Or they think it would upset Terri because everything about me upsets her. Or maybe they just didn't see it because it wasn't on the cover.

Stop it, Joanna. Just stop it.

Five letters appeared in the *City Rag* about my story. I am very pleased.

Most of the letters were complimentary. One woman wrote: "Unlike others, this piece got to the crux of the matter. The problem of gentrification has as much to do with morale as it does with economics. Even if you can afford to remain in a gentrified community, you lose your pride in that community when the newcomers take over and become the new standard-bearers." A man wrote, "It's refreshing to read an article that gets to the heart of this touchy subject." The only negative letter was from a lady who said she had been living in the Shaw neighborhood for all her 81 years and never had any trouble with whites and she for one is thrilled to death to see some new faces to "uplift" the neighborhood. I was happy to see that letter too, because if you don't irritate at least one person you haven't done your job.

I'm still waiting for a certain little someone to call. But I'm less stressed about it, now that I got some positive feedback. She's not the only person in this town, for God's sake.

And five hundred bucks doesn't hurt my mood, either. I got the check today. I know the *City Rag* doesn't pay as much as mainstream publications like *The Washingtonian,* but I prefer writing for the edgier ones. If I had a bunch of kids to support, like my dad did, I would do what he did, and get a steady job that pays good money. My dad was a newspaperman, but after *The News* folded he went into P.R. and spent the next 20 years taking us all on nice vacations and to five-star restaurants. But I don't have any kids and I don't need to spend my life making bloated companies richer.

Poor dad. Not one of his kids turned out as well-off as he was. We're all poor, some of us are drug-addled, and others are mentally ill. It's not funny, Joanna. Stop laughing. Dad always says, "I'm proud of every one of you kids." Maybe he means that we're all good people. No, that's mom's thing. "All my kids are good people." Dad's proud of how scrappy we are in spite of our problems, and he's proud of our creativity and writing abilities. And actually that's a big deal to me. After he told me my piece was "excellent," all the other compliments were just gravy.

Finally, she called me. It's about time. Yesterday afternoon the phone rang and I answered it and heard that voice, "Knadel?" Of course my heart started slamming against my chest, but then she told me that she and Sandra broke up last week, and I felt as though I could lift off and hover over the room all aglow, like a toy space ship. What a monster I am, to take delight in someone's misfortune!

Of course, she didn't rave about my article. She doesn't rave about anything I do. She said that I made it sound as though racial tension was unique to Washington, and that in her experience, DC is more "comfortably diverse" than many other cities. I never suggested that racial tension was unique to Washington, but everyone knows that DC is burbling with it right now. Maybe she hasn't experienced racial tension because she *looks* like a light-skinned black girl and black people think she's black. No, that's not it. She's just oblivious in a funny way. She's the only woman I know, besides myself, who is comfortable being the only white person in a club, restaurant, or other gathering like the Caribbean street festival. She hangs around the Islander restaurant and schmoozes with the Trinidadian owner. I can't imagine that she's unaware of how black people feel about gentrification. I'm sure she is, but I think she just needs to criticize me, no matter what I do. She did say my article was well-written, but that's like saying, "Joanna, you have a nose on your face." I don't need her to tell me *that*. She's lucky I love her, or she wouldn't get away with being all persnickety about my article.

I really shouldn't be so euphoric about her calling more than a whole *week* after my story came out. I should be highly insulted, in fact. But I'm not. I'm three feet off the ground. Wait a minute. My house buddies are talking trash out on the porch and I'm going to yell something to them.

I just yelled, "Hey! Watch your language down there! There are ladies in the house!" And little Guillermo yelled back, "Hi, Joanna!" Just that sweet greeting made my heart soar. Life is good. The sun is shining and I feel as though I've just been released from a torture chamber. All because Terri broke up with that woman. I hate to say it, but if she had praised my article to the skies but was still going with Sandra, her call would have meant nothing to me. I am so unevolved it's frightening.

We're going dancing tomorrow at Phase One, the lesbian bar down near Eastern Market. I hope it goes well. I can never predict. That's what makes me so nervous all the time. Not that I wasn't nervous before I met her. I've always been nervous, as you've probably figured out by now. When I was a real little kid, I used to blink. They should have taken me to a shrink. Actually they *did* take me to a shrink, but it wasn't because I blinked, it was because

Karen's mom called them to report that I was snatching kids' hats off in the playground and she had found pieces of paper with penises drawn all over them, so my parents schlepped me to this child therapist to show that they weren't negligent. Privately they never thought anything was wrong with me at all. And they never changed their opinion.

I'm okay now. Everything is okay. I know just because I had sex with my horrid wench last night, it doesn't mean I'm going to live happily ever after. But damn, it was good. In fact, it was the best time I've ever had in my life. It was certainly the best time I've ever had with *her*. I think everything will be okay with us now. I hope so anyway. I didn't move all the way to DC to count the water spots in this little blue room.

She was waiting for me at Phase One last night, sitting at the bar in a red shirt and black pants and one of her vests. She looked nervous, but she gave me one of her emotional hugs, the way she does after a disaster happens which, in this case, was breaking up with that idiot Sandra. After we had a couple of drinks, she told me the whole saga and I am sheepish to admit I reveled in her acerbic remarks about the woman's pathologies. I was right! She did keep getting up in the middle of dinner to throw up! At least, that's what Terri conjectured, because she stayed away from the table for a real long time and then when she returned she would be kind of sick-looking. Also, in bed she kept talking about how she still "has to get used to" being with a woman. This woman is about as gay as John Wayne.

Terri and I drank some cosmopolitans, and then we sat down and a cute young guy who was with some women friends sat down at our table (asking first if it was okay) and we were all blithering and blathering and the kid happened to mention that he was high on Ecstasy and he had some extras. Neither of us had ever done Ecstasy before. We looked at each other and I said, "Let's do some!" I must have been crazy—I haven't done drugs seriously in years—but sometimes you just get that urge. So we popped a couple E's and sailed away. Ecstasy is the most gorgeous drug. At first it made me nervous, but then we were dancing and all of a sudden I felt full—just full—full of my own life. I was pure liquefied energy. Terri and I started dancing in perfect coordination—we could have won a dance contest, we were so in synch.

During one song we did a little pirouette and I swung back around and nimbly kissed her and said, "I want to make love to you." She got this little twinkle in her eye and said, "Oh you do, do you?" We paid our bill and drove in our separate cars to her building, both of us going about 60 miles per hour. I thought I was going to lose it, trying to find a place to park, but I found a space right away. We stormed into Terri's place, tore off our clothes, and fucked on her living room rug and on the couch and half on the rug and half on the couch, for hours. Simultaneously, using our fingers and hands—not any of this "you do me and I'll do you." We moved as a single gyrating entity, trying different positions, standing up and sixty-nine and me in the back and her in the back and side-by-side and one configuration that I don't think I could ever re-create. Afterwards we went to her room and slept in each other's arms all night. And this morning she brought me breakfast in bed—eggs over easy, rye toast, and orange juice without pulp. She remembered how I like everything. She even put cream and sugar in my coffee. What a good girl!

I hope she wasn't all happy and glowy this morning just because she had sex. I know she loves sex, but I hope that her high spirits had something to do with being with me. I know I was happy and glowy from being with her. I didn't even feel much of a hangover from our wild adventure. I left around noon and I've been buzzing around all day. I think she is really going to want to be with me now. Why would she want to be with anyone else? I lived out all my fantasies last night and I am so grateful to my baby that I am going to send her some flowers. I'll send her a big spray of daffodils.

Nobody I've told about last night sounded too happy about it. Kimba and a couple of my friends from Cleveland sounded concerned, as though I'd said I'd been hearing voices telling me to jump off the roof, and Bette was even worse, acting overtly solicitous like a psychiatric nurse. Jerome just repeated his mantra that Terri's a "player." The only one who made me feel good was Guillermo, who lit up when I told him and said, "That's wonderful, honey! I hope everything works out!" The other ones just don't get it. Do they know what it's like when someone walks into your life and fills up all the dry, empty spaces? The pop psychologists say the songs on the radio aren't true. They say a relationship can't save you, that you have to feel tippity-top by yourself. And when I think of how I swallowed all that for years, I want to scream. Because it turns out that *they* were wrong and the *songs* were right. You *can't* feel tippity-top by yourself. And a relationship *can* save you. You see it happen all the time.

Terri called to thank me for the flowers. She was so perfunctory about it you'd have thought I had just returned her vacuum cleaner. That's so typical of her. She invited me to a "play party" hosted by an organization called "Sexual Exploration by Women," abbreviated to SEXX. It's a women's leather group in Virginia. I've never been to a play party. All I know is that these leather women are into acting out S&M fantasies. Maybe Terri will tie me up at the party and do things to me while I scream and plead with her to "Please stop! Please stop!" That would be the tits. I hope *she* initiates it. I don't want to *ask* to be rendered helpless. That would defeat the whole purpose.

The most lovely breeze is wafting through my screened windows. Birds are chirping, cars are sailing by, and the moist air is hugging me like an aunt you don't see very often, a pleasant hug, not enveloping like a grandmother's hug. That will happen in August, people tell me. They say, just wait. It gets really bad here in August. But they don't know me. Just as I loved my grandmother's hugs, I love a humid day. Without humidity, it just ain't summer.

I would never want air conditioning. I love my little room with my screened windows. Screens are among my favorite things. I can still hear the screen door slam when we used to run in and out of the house when we were kids. I'm talking about the old house, our little brick house on Lawson Drive, before we moved to the Big House (as Tommy calls it) and got central air and I started to feel trapped in.

Joanna, just go to the store.

I know I'm avoiding thinking about the future. I'm so used to chasing a butterfly that I don't know what I'll do once it's in my hand. Can we really live together? When I fell in love with her, I was ready to throw all my stuff in the proverbial U-Haul and move in with her. I could have lived in a broom closet with her. But now I don't know how it would work. She's very practical and down-to-earth, and she's critical and tactless and often not even nice. How could I live with her, let alone be her partner in life?

But I can be her partner in life. I want to be her partner in life. I just don't know if I could live with her. Is that a contradiction?

She could have been a little sweeter about the flowers, the little twit. Maybe I should tie *her* up at that party and do things to *her*. That would give me a great deal of pleasure.

That play party was ridiculous. I would have had more fun going to the Safeway.

The party was in a ranch house on a nondescript street in Fairfax, Virginia. A woman who looked like Morticia in the Addams Family opened the door and showed us to the living room, where a lot of really skinny or really fat women were drifting around in sailor and police uniforms and leather garments. They all looked tentative and insecure and alone. It felt like a "getting acquainted" gathering for employees of some bizarre company. We had no idea where the hostess was, or even if the hostess was on the premises, and we never did solve that mystery.

Most of the "action" took place in the living room, where a skinny naked butch woman lay on a massage table having saltwater squirted into her vagina by a straight-looking blonde woman. A few women stood there watching. It was so silly. The "victim" and the "torturer" were chattering to each other as though they were sitting in a kitchen having tea. Whenever the water torture got a little rough and the butch woman twitched or winced, the blond woman turned into a cheer leader, cooing things like, "Just a little bit more now," and "You're doing so well!" Terri said in her tactless fashion, "What is this, an S&M scene or a Lamaze class?" and I had to pretend I didn't know her. Someone next to us said the blond woman was a "professional" from California, and Terri said, "If she's a professional dominatrix, we're all in trouble." I thought that was a good time to walk away, so I went to another scene taking place in the corner of the room. A frizzy-haired girl lay on a mat in her underpants while a crewcutted tomboy leaned over her, pushing and stretching and otherwise manipulating her arms and legs. Terri came over and watched, and I said "What are they supposed to be doing?" and Terri said, "Maybe she's practicing kneading dough," and I started laughing so hard that we had to leave. We peaked into the next room, where an enormous woman was strapped to a whipping post while someone who looked like her identical twin whipped her back with a toy whip like the kind you find in those "pleasure" shops. Their expressions were completely blank. Terri said, "Hm. Tenderizing meat," which made me lose it again.

As a last resort we went into the dining room, where the table was laid out with an imaginative platter of celery, carrots, and cauliflower, French onion dip and humus. The accompaniment was red punch. I asked a sailor woman if there was any beer and she said they don't allow alcohol at these parties, I suppose because someone might get drunk and ram a hose up someone's gigi and not be able to get it out.

We left without eating. All the way home we laughed

and made fun of the party, but I felt kind of disappointed. I thought maybe we would end up doing some kind of kinky scene in there, but the event had all the eroticism of a children's piano recital. Also I felt strangely deflated about Terri taking me there in the first place. I want her to make love with me. Nobody's ever made love with me before, being sweet and tender with me all night and then the two of us lying in bed the whole next day, drinking mimosas and cuddling. The other night was wonderful, but it wasn't what you'd call making love. It was just fucking. The fact that Terri took me to that party before she's made love to me makes me feel kind of bad.

Cherry Hill is dust in the wind.

She asked me to lunch, and we met at the café behind Kramer Books. We had talked to each other a couple of times on the phone, but we hadn't seen each other since that one climactic meeting a couple weeks ago. She greeted me excitedly, and we sat outside in the tropical heat chatting about this and that, but she could tell something was amiss. When we were done eating, I told her I saw Terri and that she's back in my life. She asked if we had sex and I hesitated, then said yes, we did, and she asked if I still love Terri and I said yes, I did. She started to cry and I yelled at her because I was so upset seeing her cry. I said she was making me feel awful and I didn't know what to do about it, and that I waited my whole life to fall in love and it meant everything to me and I no longer want to have sex with people I'm not in love with. I started to add, "even though you're one of the sexiest babes I've ever known," but before I could say that she got up and ran out through the exit and down the street.

I feel terrible. I keep seeing her hurrying down the street in her little pumps, her yellow dress clinging to her doughy body, the tears pouring from her eyes. I had made her happy, and then I deflated her. We only had one date, but we jumped right into bed, and that can do you in. Maybe we shouldn't have done it, but my God it was fun. I will always remember that afternoon. I hope that she'll remember it fondly, too, after she gets over my being a jerk with her. But she probably won't. All she'll remember is my wounding her to the core. Except I'm sure she'll have the good sense to get over it in a few days, unlike moi, who never gets over being hurt and just keeps flying back like a beanbag against a wall.

I wonder if Cherry will tell Judge Holmes that I treated her shoddily. I hope not, because that would piss Louise off royally, especially after she herself put me in touch with Cherry, and if I ever appear before her again she might send me to some prison hellhole to be eaten alive by the she-wolves. Kimba said she might even *hire* someone to go in there and do the job. I asked her how she would get them in there and she looked at me kind of cross-eyed like, How can you be so stupid. And I said, Oh yeah, she's a judge. She can do anything. And Kimba said "Yeah-eah!" the way she says it, in a sarcastic sing-song. Kimba is so funny.

She's also very sweet. She told me that Cherry is responsible for her own actions, she's not a child and I shouldn't feel bad because she'll get over it. She said Cherry has broken hearts and now it was her turn to have her heart broken and it's just how things go. She's right, but I can't get that image out of my mind, of Cherry trotting down the street in her yellow frock, the tassels on her purse flapping frantically like teeny little arms.

July 2000

Kimba, Bette, and I arranged to meet Terri, Terri's friend Linda, and a friend of Linda's for drinks yesterday at the Playbill on 14th Street. And Linda's friend turned out to be, lo and behold, Dee Williams! I swear I've never seen such an enclosed community in my life since I came out and joined the lesbos. Dee greeted me with a warm hug and kiss, and I felt completely forgiven for my behavior during that goofy date of ours. The whole bunch of us sat in a comfortable alcove on couches and drank the night away. Everyone got really drunk except, I think, Kimba.

Terri and I sat catty-corner to each other on separate love seats, and even though my wench had her leg draped over me she spent most of the night talking to Dee. It's typical of her to focus her attention on some new person that she doesn't know. She's always good with new people, but then, after she gets to know them, she gets sick of them. Anyway, we had a good time. Among us we probably drank about 20 cosmopolitans. I discovered that I like mine with Cointreau rather than Triple Sec. It's much smoother that way. I turned Kimba onto that version and she loved it, especially because she hates Triple

Sec. Terri, in her typical ornery fashion, tried one cosmo with Cointreau and then the next one she ordered with Triple Sec. I got really upset, I hate to admit it. I was seriously bummed out for about 10 minutes that she didn't love my version of the Cosmopolitan.

Dee is funny and pretty and sassy and has that endearing immaturity that many gay people have because they began their adolescence late—when they came out rather than when they physically mature. I joked with her about our date and told her I buried those cigarettes under a bench, and she laughed and laughed. We talked about her job and she said she was pleased that her field of child advocacy was growing. She said she loved my article in the *City Rag* and was impressed with the "vibrancy" of my writing, which made her my friend for life.

Bette warned me that Terri was flirting with Dee, but I don't think she was. I think she was just doing her typical thing of getting to know her. She always chats up new people, and has an affinity with black women, as I do. Also Terri is naturally charming in small groups, even though she's shy. Shy people can be extremely charming because they try harder. Not that anyone would ever know Terri was shy. She comes across like a brick falling on your head. She's more comfortable speaking in front of people, where she can be the center of attention, than in small social groups where you're supposed to just fit yourself in.

Maybe I'll call Dee to get together. The funny thing is, I feel kind of hesitant to do that, because it will seem as though I'm making a play for her. But it's as natural for me to pursue friendships as it is for most people to pursue romantic relationships. And it's especially nice to be friends with attractive women that you might even go out with if you didn't love someone else.

Speaking of that, I invited Terri to come over Friday night, since she's never seen my place. We're going to watch some of the *Twilight Zone* marathon on my little TV. I'm hoping they'll show the one about the evil kid Anthony who reads people's minds and if he doesn't like what they're thinking he zaps them into the cornfield. Terri and I both get a kick out of that one because it takes place in a town in Ohio, which somehow snapped off from the rest of the planet and whirled into the Twilight Zone. Of course, we may be too distracted by other things (wink wink!) to concentrate on the antics of demonic TV children. (Take out "wink wink." That's just awful. I know, but I'm going to leave it in anyway. At least I didn't say, "hubba hubba." I had a male friend in New York who used to say "hubba hubba" and I got rid of him. Well, I got rid of him after he subjected me to an awful Ingmar Bergman movie, but "hubba hubba" had already set the stage for his demise.)

I'm very nervous to have Terri see this dumpy house and all my weird friends. What if she disapproves of my living among "street people"? But they're not really street people because they're living somewhere, even if it is a dumpy rooming house. At the very least, they're high-functioning street people. I shouldn't look down on them anyway because I'm turning into a derelict myself. I hardly work or eat anymore. All I do is lie on this bed and think about having sex with Terri. I keep trying to remember that position when we were half on the couch and half on the floor, because I burst like a bottle rocket while we were doing it and I would like to do it again. As I said, I've become totally useless. Kimba says my theme song is that one that goes "I don't wanna work! I just wanna bang on my drum all day!" She's right. She's very, very right.

Terri's visit to my place was a disaster. I never should have invited her over here. It was bad enough that she saw half the population of this place eating at a mission. Now her impression of my living situation has become reinforced by this idiotic scene that occurred right under her nose.

It started the moment I let her in the front door. As the two of us passed one of the rooms, we heard yelling, and I realized it was the room belonging to Fred, the big silent guy with the marbled face that I'd never heard a peep from the whole time I'd been living here. Then the door flew open and there was Fred literally flinging this smarmy-looking white guy out the door, and the white guy crashed right into Terri, who went reeling, and then he ran to the exit, and Fred yelled after him, "Mother-fucker, you'd better run, 'cause I got something that can blow a hole in you bigger than your Elmer Fudd head!" Terri recovered herself and I hustled her upstairs, and there was busybody Jerome eavesdropping over the banister, and he said, "They're at it again, I see." Again?, I thought. I barely knew the man existed before then.

Then Jerome smiled suggestively at Terri and drawled, "Well, hello, Terri," in this buttery voice, and Terri said hello in a not very friendly voice, and then that dopey transvestite, Calliope, came shuffling upstairs. She is a sight to behold, with her plunging red satin dress and satin shoes and dangling earrings (Terri probably thought she looked hot), and Calliope looked at Terri and said, "What are *you* lookin' at?" I introduced Terri to her, and Terri said "*Calliope?*" because she didn't like being dissed. Calliope glared at Terri, put her hand on her hip, whirled around, and strutted into Jerome's room, where they would spend the next several hours watching Jerry Springer and other highbrow fare.

We lay on my bed and watched about four *Twilight Zones*. I don't know how Terri managed to lie on a single bed without touching me, but she did. She lay against the pillow with her arms at her sides, not really hanging off the bed but leaving a good couple inches of space between us that I could not penetrate and didn't even dare. I opened a bottle of wine and we drank practically the whole thing and I may have been sipping on dishwater, with all the effect it had on me. They did show our favorite *Twilight Zone* about Anthony the evil mind-reading boy who zaps people into the cornfield, but I felt the most unnerving identification with the zapped people and it made me feel very creepy. The other reruns were good too—they showed "Talky Tina" about the doll who ends up killing the child's mean father, the one about the woman who is chased through a department store by mannequins and who turns out to be an escaped mannequin herself, and that classic about the ugly, deformed woman who submits to plastic surgery, and when they take off the bandages everyone is horrified because it didn't work, and then you see her for the first time and she looks like Marilyn Monroe and all the doctors and nurses look like pigs.

After we got tired of the *Twilight Zones,* I channel-surfed, but there was nothing on. We just lay there awkwardly, and finally Terri said, "Do you want to talk about the other night?" and I said, "Not really," afraid of what she would say. She said, "Well, thanks for having me over," and sat up and put on her shoes on. Then she got up, stood over me, tweaked me on the nose, and said, "It was the drug." I wanted to kill her. I walked her downstairs and she tipped an imaginary hat to me and walked out the door. I stood there, hating her and hating myself and hating that asinine Fred who made Terri think I'm living in some kind of low-rent hovel. I'm sure that's part of the reason she made that stinging comment about our sexual encounter being all about "the drug." I don't even want to think about the other part.

You know what? The hell with her. I'm going to walk up to this new place on 18th Street and drink. I discovered something there called a "sidecar." It's a classic old drink made with brandy, triple sec, and sour mix, and it sends you to the moon. I need to be on the moon right now. Terri always makes me feel as though my life is one big embarrassment. I've lost all my old brio. Why can't she ever cut me a break? It wasn't my fault that stupid Fred had a hissy fit in front of her. If I'm not absolutely perfect, she decides I'm no good at all. I'm not talking to her anymore. She can fry in hell.

Well, I recovered from my attack of sanity about Terri and went right back to talking to her, but there's no rest for the wicked. We were gabbing yesterday about this and that and she just mentioned in passing that she called Dee. She got her car tuned up, the cat knocked down her mom's picture, Tiny isn't speaking to her, she called Dee Williams. I'm assuming she just wants to be friendly, because Terri is a big networker, and I know she liked Dee. But it bugged me because *I* wanted to call Dee. And Terri beat me to the punch. So not only am I jealous of *Dee*, but I'm jealous of *Terri*. It's awful. It's just awful.

I asked Kimba what she thought about Terri calling Dee and Kimba said, "Maybe she wants to date her." I wish Kimba hadn't *said* that. Even though I don't think it's true (Terri just said they talked about the conflict between lesbians and transgendered women), now I'm very uneasy because Kimba is always right. Like, if she said, "I think President Clinton is gay," it would turn out that he really is gay. I told Jerome what Kimba said and he agreed with her. He said, "She's going after her. Stop dreaming and find yourself a woman you can trust." He said I should start dating Kimba. But I don't love Kimba, I love Terri. What am I supposed to do? Go to one of those neuro-linguistic programmers who snaps people out of things? I don't even *want* to snap out of loving the bitch.

Anyway, is Terri screwing Dee Williams? No. All she did was call her. So everyone should just shut up about it. That's what I said to Kimba, who replied in her soft little teasing voice, "*Who* should shut up about it?"

That shut me up. At least for a few minutes. Then I started talking about it again.

August 2000

Terri said she and Dee have been "seeing each other" for a couple of weeks. Okay, fine. I'm perfectly okay with this. At least Dee is a worthy opponent. Most of the women Terri's dated since I've met her are total duds and I always think, Why on earth would she prefer *her* to *me*? She must consider me something that crawled out from under a rock. But Dee Williams is smart and attractive and classy and even someone *I* would date, so at least I'm not insulted that she's dating Dee even though I wish she were dating me instead.

Actually what bothers me most is that *I* had wanted to call Dee and hang out with her and now I can't because it will look as though I'm butting in. *I* was the one Dee was interested in originally. When we went out for drinks, we had a wonderful discussion about her child advocacy, and all Terri did was make little comments about the straps on her shoes and the way she ate olives. But now that I think about it, who's going to get the girl's attention, the one who expounds to her about intellectual matters or the one who leans over and murmurs, "You like to tease your olives before you swallow them, don't you?" I didn't hear her say that, but Kimba did. She tried to warn me.

Maybe I should have listened to Kimba. But even if I did, what could I have done? Terri will always do what she wants to do. In fact, she will always most likely do the exact opposite of what I *want* her to do.

But I can't let it get to me. I just can't. Terri is probably just trying to make me jealous. Not that she doesn't like Dee. But how much can she like her? She doesn't even know her. She's just attracted to her at the moment. She's always attracted to the new and fresh. It's my fault for not acting soon enough. If I had called Dee, Terri would have stayed away. I'm so slow to act on things, and then I end up out in the cold while two people that *I* want to be with hook up with *each other*. Anyway, I want Terri to do as she pleases. I love her and I want her to be happy. Not that I want her to be happy with someone other than myself, but it's futile to go against the flow of things. This is all in the flow of things. So let it be, Joanna. Just let it be.

Maybe I should get some new shoes. That's what I need. I'm going to the mall right now. I'll go to PG Mall, because I can take the Metro and not have to change trains. I don't trust my driving right now. I feel kind of bummed out about this Dee thing. I said I wasn't, but I am. I'll feel better after I get some shoes. That's exactly what I need. These shoes are not sexy. They're clunky. Why didn't I notice it before? I hate these shoes. I can't believe I even bought them.

Next week is Terri's birthday, and I have planned a nice evening for us, at her place. We're going to order pizza and I'll bring a bottle of wonderful vintage wine that I bought when the two of us went to the Ohio Wine Festival years ago, which I've been saving for a special occasion. I bought her the most fetching glass figure of a woman holding a little torch. She can add it to her prized glass collection in her mother's china cabinet. We'll eat the pizza, drink the wine, and get cozy.

I'm assuming her thing with Dee isn't exactly going like gangbusters, or she would not have been so amenable to this plan when I proposed it. If she and Dee were still an item, wouldn't Terri want to spent her birthday with *her*? Kimba said that maybe Dee has a class that night, but I don't think that's the case. What *I* think is that Terri just wants to spend her birthday with me, and not with Dee. I'm going to use the occasion of her birthday to put my cards on the table. I'm going to tell her that I love her and that we could be very good together and that we should put all the craziness behind us and have a fresh start. I haven't actually done that yet. I've just been whirling and whirling around her like a dervish. Or like a sputnik, as Tommy would say. I need to be an adult with her for once in my life. I *am* an adult, after all. Well, I used to be an adult. I don't know what the hell I am now. Try coming out when you're in your forties. It turns you into some kind of hybrid—part woman, part unrecognizable creature like one of those funny monsters that kids watch on TV that nobody can even identify because they've never seen anything like it.

September 2000

Terri's birthday celebration wasn't what I had hoped. In fact, it was dreadful beyond belief. I don't want to stop writing. I'm writing, writing, writing. I'm afraid of what will happen if I stop.

I wanted so badly to have a sweet, intimate evening with Terri on her birthday. I wanted it to be cathartic. Well, maybe it was cathartic, but it was cathartic the other way. When I was on my way to pick up the gourmet pizza, Terri called on my cell phone and said that she had "expanded" her birthday plans and invited Kimba, Linda, and Dee. (She didn't invite Bette, I think because she senses Bette's fierce protectiveness of me.) Terri sounded extremely nervous over the phone, I suppose thinking I would say, "Well then, fuck you, I'm not coming." I was making my way through traffic, so I couldn't process the reality of what she was saying, which was that she didn't want to have an intimate evening with me because Dee was in her life. So instead of telling her what to do with these new birthday plans, I exclaimed, "That's great! We'll have fun!" I may as well have said, "Thank you, sir! May I have another?"

Dee hugged me gratefully when I walked into Terri's place, as though to say, "I so appreciate you're being a good sport about all this". During the gathering Kimba, Linda, and I sat on Terri's living room floor, and Terri and Dee sat on the couch holding hands. The bitch obviously worked some kind of spell on Dee because she was glowing like one of those frisky, frolicking maidens in a museum painting. After a few minutes, Terri opened her presents—she's like a little kid with presents; she can't wait. When she opened my present, she pulled the glass figurine out of the box, looked at me and nodded, and said, "Thank you, Knadel." When she opened Dee's present, which was a watch, she looked into Dee's eyes and kissed her. Kimba and Linda were sitting there the whole evening, looking uncomfortable and feeling sorry for me. I sat there like a statue the whole night except when I got up a couple of times to get pizza and go to the bathroom. I tried to be pleasant and in the spirit of a birthday party, but I drew the line at eating the chocolate cake Dee made with an orange happy face, which was making me sick just to look at it. I politely declined when Dee offered me a slice and Terri looked at me sharply; the woman doesn't miss a thing.

Around nine o'clock, Terri started making a big show of carting the dishes to the kitchen. Linda said, "Is this a hint for us to leave?" and Terri said emphatically, "It's about that time." She was referring to all of us but Dee, who, when we were leaving, stood at the door next to Terri, kissing everyone goodbye like the lady of the house. I kissed her warmly like the fake that I am and I hugged Terri, who hugged me back stiffly. I walked to the Metro with Kimba, who chattered away about the full moon and something about some of the planets being more visible than in the last million years; one thing about Kimba is that she never asks me if I'm upset. She waits for me to bring it up. But I didn't want to talk about it. I'm dealing with it on my own. I'm fine. I'm perfectly all right.

This thing with Dee won't last long. Terri's little relationships never last very long. Believe me, she won't be spending her next birthday with Dee. She'll be spending it with—well, maybe not me, but with someone else. I don't give a shit who she spends it with. I don't care if she ever has a birthday again.

That's a terrible thing to say. I didn't mean it. Well, I did mean it. I feel bad meaning it. I hate hating her. I hate hating anyone. I definitely don't hate Dee. I just feel like such a jackass, like I missed some kind of opportunity with her, even though I love stupid Terri. I feel like a ninny. Why couldn't I have called Dee the day after we met for drinks? Terri makes moves and I just sit on my ass and write in this pathetic diary that will probably end just as Tommy and I humorously predicted, with me running naked down Connecticut Avenue, tearing out my hair, and ending up on a loony ward.

I'm going to stop writing because I have to go to work. It's Saturday and I need to work because people will be home. I need to stop this moping and kick into my work mode. It's not as though someone died or anything. Do you hear me, Joanna? Nobody *died*.

I just got back from work. It was the worst day of work that I've ever had. I couldn't get anyone to talk to me. The whole time I was out there, I was feeling like a rabbit about to be devoured by a lion—weak and shaky and terrified and doomed. This is ridiculous. I will not allow it to continue. I have *always* been able to function! Always! No matter what is happening in my life, I work. I write. I talk. I survive. I do not lose control. Even when I was a kid setting fires, I did it with the specific purpose of getting sent away so I could be rescued and also to cultivate an identity as a crazy kid. It's not in my nature to completely lose control. Dee Williams or no Dee Williams, I need to pull myself together.

If anyone had seen me today out in the field, they would have thought I was a mental case out practicing her "life skills." The nightmare started in the Northeast ghetto of Trinidad. I went to a little house with an American flag and a man with a 60s-style Afro came out and I started talking to him in a teeny-weeny little voice, and he said, "I don't know what you want, Miss, but you ain't gettin' any," and he slammed the door in my face. At the next house a grandmother was standing there with two little kids and I started to squeak something about the study and she said, "I don't want to get into all that mess," and shut the door. At the third house a young woman saw me through the screen door and she came over and said "I don't have time," and I whimpered that I only needed a few minutes, but she was already walking away. I started to go into a panic and left Trinidad and drove across town to Cleveland Park. The rich people were even meaner than the ghetto people, and I started to lose it. One woman said, "You shouldn't go knocking on people's doors," and I yelled, "That's the way the study is *designed*," and she shut the door on me. I went to another house and a college-aged boy was walking out the door and started to answer questions on his porch, and then he interrupted the interview and looked at me and said, "You should go home and get some sleep." Then he trotted off down the street, leaving me standing on his porch like an idiot. At that point I should have gone home, but I dragged over to a house with a mezuzah on it and banged on the door until a middle-aged man answered and he looked at me as though I were Hermann Goering and said *"Vut do you vant?"* and I started to tell him and he said "I'm sorry," and shut the door, and I banged on it again until he opened it, and I started yelling that he lived in his own little world and he should realize that he was part of a community—I think I said "goddam community," and that it was no skin off his nose to give me a couple minutes of his time. He said he was going to call the police and shut the door again, and I was too furious to go home, so I drove to a fancy building on Columbia

Road that I got kicked out of last week by this desk guard that thinks she's an army sergeant, and I marched into the ornate lobby and told her that I needed to talk to these people and if she didn't let me through I would wait outside for them to come home. She said, "I can't allow that," but I ignored her and went to my car and hauled a beach chair out of my trunk and parked it in front of the building and sat on it, and I admit I looked foolish sitting in front of this luxury building in my little yellow beach chair, and in ten minutes the police came and I explained my business there and they said too bad, I couldn't sit out there. I said if it was any building other than "The Fucking Wyoming" they wouldn't even have bothered to come and they told me if I didn't leave immediately I would be under arrest and I picked up my beach chair and started to fold it and squeezed my finger in it and said, "Goddam son of a bitch!" and one of the cops said, "Watch your language, Miss" and I muttered, "Fuck you" and left.

I can't stand this. I have to do something. I know what I'll do. Tomorrow I'll go to Terri's and try to talk some sense into her. I know that sounds crazy. But I love her. We had such a nice time that night when we had sex in her living room in all those positions and then went to sleep in each other's arms. Why wouldn't she want to do it again? Not take Ecstasy again, but just spend some time together, making love and eating and drinking mimosas and cuddling and laughing and talking. I don't understand why she doesn't want to do that with me.

I didn't eat again today. I know that's bad.

(*You know it's bad? Of course it's bad! You are going to drop over from hunger! Do you want to end up in the hospital?*

172

—Oh please, mother. Please. I don't have time for this.

Never mind you don't have time for it! What kind of a person goes all day without eating? How much weight have you lost?

—Twelve pounds.

Twelve pounds? You are wasting away to nothing. Nothing!)

I can't help it. I can't eat. I keep picturing that chocolate cake with the orange happy face on it and I go to the bathroom and retch into the toilet. It's already happened three times today.

Kimba and Bette are sitting here, making me write. They dragged this diary over to the hospital along with my toothbrush and pajamas and dumped it on my lap, telling me it will help keep me sane while I'm here. I'm in the hospital not from not eating, like my mom threatened, but because I crashed the car and I'm lying here all beat up. I can't believe I did it. I never get into accidents. I'm an excellent driver, just like Raymond in *Rain Man*. I think I have gone crazy. I'm afraid I'm going to die after I leave here. Kimba said, "Well, we're all going to die eventually," and Bette reprimanded her and said, "Don't worry, honey, we won't let you die." But Bette and Kimba can't be with me every second of the day. They do have to work, after all.

I can't believe it was only this morning that the phone woke me and Wanda, my supervisor, was on the other end, telling me there were two complaints called in about me. One was from the Jewish guy and the other from the army sergeant at the Wyoming. Instead of being contrite I said, "Tough shit." Wanda told me we would discuss it later and hung up the phone. I was too agitated to keep sleeping, so I got up and got dressed and walked over to Terri's. She was expressionless when she saw me and the whole time I was visiting she treated me like a magazine saleswoman. She spoke to me in a formal voice and called me "Joanna" instead of "Knadel." She asked about my car, if I'd gotten the brakes fixed. I said I did, and it cost me $300. She asked me how my job was going and I lied and said it was going okay, and then we didn't have anything more to talk about, but I just kept sitting there. I was feeling so hurt and desperate that I blurted out, "Why don't we get married?" and it was supposed to be kind of a joke, but she got annoyed and said coldly, "That's not in the plans." Pretty soon after that I got up in defeat, and she ushered me out of her apartment.

I walked home stiffly, feeling like a very old woman, and trudged up the steps and went into the house, and there was a package from my mom in the mail pile. She had told me she was sending me an anthology of Cleveland Orchestra performances conducted by the great George Szell. She was so excited about it. Seeing the box gave me a little lift, a feeling of being loved. I remembered that I needed some milk, so I ran across the street to the store, and when I returned ten minutes later, the package was gone. I started charging through the house, demanding to know if anyone knew where it was. I ran up the stairs and some thugs walked out of Jerome's room and I asked them if they had seen my package and they looked away from me and one of them said, "I don't even know what you're talking about," and I figured that one of them had it hidden in his baggy pants, but there was nothing I could do and they trotted down the stairs.

Then I went on a rampage, screaming at everyone in the hall that I was sick of people stealing credit cards and stealing food from the refrigerator and now somebody ripped off my fucking CDs and I'm going to kick their fucking ass, and I kicked the walls a few times and then I grabbed a lamp that was sitting on a table in the hall and threw it across the hall and it broke. Then I decided that I would find those thugs who took my CDs and follow them to see where they tried to sell them and I stormed out of the house and sped down T Street, and a woman was crossing the street and I saw her too late and cut the wheel and crashed into a fireplug. My head hit the dashboard and my chest went into the steering wheel and now I'm lying in Howard University Hospital with broken ribs and my face looking like Times Square and my car is all crashed up, but I'm tanked up on Demerol, so I don't care. In fact, I'm surprisingly chipper for someone who just had a car accident. I wouldn't mind staying here for a few weeks, or even a few months. What's not to like? They even gave me my own room.

I can't believe what a loser I turned out to be. This wasn't supposed to happen to me. I was an *enfant terrible* reaching for the brass ring. And now look at me! Almost fifty years old, living in a rooming house with nuts and weirdos, practically broke, with nobody to love me. Lying in a hospital after going berserk and crashing the car. I'm like one of those scraggly women people take out to lunch and talk to them about how to get their lives on track, and give them a list of resources with names like Bertha's Room and Hands Across the Water.

I refuse to go to Hands Across the Water. I won't. I'd

rather live on the streets, which I will be soon if I can't work.

Good God. I just got it. Those people out there, *they* were like *me* not too long ago. Living in hovels, one step from the streets. And once they were *on* the streets, *they* refused to go to "Hands Across the Water" too. And that's why they're on the streets—because, like me, they still have their pride and refuse to accept help from pitying people who see what they have become. You have to lose all your pride if you want to rise from the bottom. And since I still have pride, my goose is cooked. I'll just keep regressing until I'm lying in a trash heap with shit on my pants.

I can't believe I'm writing this drivel. I should throw it away before someone sees it. Kimba is sitting on the chair eating a moon pie, but Bette is hovering around my bed, fluffing the pillows and she might try to peek. On the other hand, she probably thinks I'm in such a piteous state that anything I write would be completely incoherent.

I just met a fellow patient and I poured myself all over him. I hope he doesn't think I'm crazy. I am in such an awful state with my concussion and broken ribs and broken heart that everything I do or say feels crazy. I don't think I can function if I leave this hospital. That's what scares me. I've never literally felt as though I was falling apart, except when I was younger and used to have panic attacks, but they would go away. This isn't going to go away. Terri doesn't want me and she never will. I can't deal with it, so I have to stay in this hospital. I'll figure out some way to do it. I like it here. I've always loved institutional food, like Salisbury steak and chicken à-la-king and peach cobbler, even though I've been too upset to eat. I like being taken care of, and except for this one harridan, all the nurses here are darling. And I have a new friend, Nicky, except maybe he thinks I'm nuts and won't talk to me anymore. That's not true. Of course he will.

He popped into my room this morning when I was lying in bed, wanting to die, this handsome guy in jeans and slippers and a hospital robe. He said, "Hi! I'm Nicky Stewart!" Then he looked at my face and exclaimed,

"Lord Jesus! What happened to you?" I never saw him before in my life, but my whole ridiculous story started pouring out of my mouth. "I never had a car accident in my life," I babbled, "but the woman I'm in love with is with someone else and I got all distraught about it and drove into a fire hydrant. But not on purpose!" I yelped, not wanting him to think I was suicidal. It was bad enough that I was obviously mentally unstable. But instead of recoiling, Nicky said, "Oh, you poor thing!" and he bopped right over to my bed and sat on it, crossing his legs, Yoga-style. For some reason, I didn't mind his familiarity. He said, "My boyfriend just left me for a Polish giant." I really didn't want to hear his troubles at the moment, but I was feeling better already from being jolted out of my morbid thoughts. "What do you mean, a giant?" I said. "Literally a giant?"

"Literally a giant," Nicky said. "Seven feet tall."

"Does he play basketball?" I asked.

"No, he's a large-animal veterinarian," Nicky said.

"Does he look up pigs' asses?" I said, and Nicky said, "Yes, both at work and at home," and I laughed. I decided that if this guy could make me laugh in the state I was in, he could sit cross-legged on my bed till doomsday. He told me he was in the hospital because he was having ferocious headaches, probably from the stress of losing his boyfriend. "I'm one of the most successful attorneys in DC and I feel like a little putz," he said. "My self-esteem is in the toilet, just from being gay. Being gay sucks. Don't you think so?"

Well, that may have been the wrong thing to ask me, because I launched into a depressive eruption that even

179

his most hysterical fag friends probably couldn't match. I told him I didn't know I was gay until a few years ago, and before that I tried not to be gay and that was even worse. I said I'd always imagined that I had a pretty cool life, because I was a writer and had all these friends and was nice-looking, at least when I was younger, and Nicky interjected, "You're nice-looking now, even underneath all of that phantasmagoria," and I decided he was going to be my friend for life. I told him that I now realized I'd been fooling myself, and that my life had really been pretty shitty, and all the supposedly cool things about it weren't cool at all, like acting up at school and setting trash can fires and getting thrown in a loony bin when I was fourteen. "I loved it in there," I said. "I didn't want to leave. I couldn't go out with girls, so I had to get my thrills from flooding the school bathrooms and setting trash fires and being locked up with a bunch of crazy people!"

"I was in a loony bin when I was fourteen!" Nicky exclaimed, and we high-fived each other. I asked him why he was in loony bin, and he said, "I licked this boy's ear when he passed me in the hall."

"Well, so what if you licked a boy's ear?" I said furiously. "Why would they put you in a loony bin for that? That's no big deal!" Once I like someone, even if I've only known him for five minutes, I become as loyal as though I were part of his family.

"He went home and told his father and his father called the principal and the principal had a meeting with my parents," Nicky said. "He told them that I sometimes engaged in odd behavior. I never forgot that. He made it

180

sound like I was some weirdo. I ended up in a bin for a week. They decided I was just this little faggot and sent me home."

"Ha!" I said. "At least they had the good sense to know you were a faggot." I told him I was in the bin for six months and nobody ever figured out I was gay. I am still astonished at the extent of the ignorance of those so-called experts. I walked with this little swagger, I wore nothing but jeans, and I flirted with all the nurses in the bin. I had crushes on half of them and followed them around like a puppy. I had no attraction to boys at all. Anyone today would have known. But back then in suburban Cleveland they were still living back in the fifties even though it was the sixties. "They thought homosexuality was an incurable disease," I said to Nicky. "If they had found out I was this little lezzie, it would have been like discovering I had inoperable cancer. 'We are so sorry to tell you, Mr. and Mrs. Kane, that your daughter is a—what did they call them?—a sexual invert!" Nicky laughed. "Of course, I was just as ignorant as the rest of them," I said. "I pictured lesbians as these pathetic women hanging around bus stations with big hollow eyes. It took me thirty years to figure out that I was one of them."

And then I went into my thing about trying to be with men my whole life and never falling in love and never even having a real relationship. "I just had sex," I said. "It was positively sordid. I fucked one man after another, because I thought I should just keep trying until something worked. I always had to be drunk. Then I would wake up the next morning and think, 'Where's my

181

goddam post-coital glow?'" Nicky listened patiently. That's the nice thing about gay people. They understand the depth of your rage. I told him that I'd been depressed my whole life and didn't even know it, that I was one of those intellectual Jewish girls who went around smoking marijuana and writing poems and discussing Herman Hesse and suppressing her libido while everyone else was falling in love and fucking their brains out. "I was like a giant head with no body attached to it," I said. "I channeled all my energy into writing, but I could only write about stuff no one could relate to. I didn't know anything about love or passion or sex. And so I ended up with no literary success, no love, and no nothing! God, I hate myself!"

Nicky asked me when I finally came out, and I told him that I had been telling people I could go both ways, but I'd never actually been with a woman, and I'd stopped having sex with men, so I was celibate. "I thought I was frigid and I loathed myself because I valued passion above everything," I told Nicky. "I started going to a massage therapist to get some relief, and I developed a crush on her. One day after a massage I went to visit my friend Ann and she said, 'How is Frances?', referring to my massage therapist. And that's when I realized I was gay. Standing in Ann's kitchen while she stirred a pot of soup. The whole room got bright and I just stood there, quieting erupting with this knowledge. I said to myself, 'Joanna, you are a lesbian. You've always been a lesbian.' I didn't say anything to Ann right then, but by the next day I was announcing it to the world. I was so happy. A lot of people didn't believe me, but eight months later I met Terri, and then they did." I laughed.

"Coming out is phenomenal," Nicky said. "When I came out I felt like Pinnochio, the wooden boy who finally stopped lying to everyone and turned into a real boy. Coming out is coming alive."

"I know!" I said. "But I didn't come alive until I was forty-five years old! I was forty-five when I was born! And now I'm going to have this short life, because even if I live to be eighty, I'll really be only thirty-five when I die!" I burst into tears and Nicky scooted up the bed and lay next to me and put his arm around me. "Terri doesn't want me and I'll never fall in love again," I sobbed. "I'll never have anyone to love me. I don't have any children and now it's too late to have them. I'm in menopause. I'm old and broken down and I'm going to end up in some musty old apartment, and I'll kick off one day and they won't find me until the neighbors complain about the smell!" I buried my face in Nicky's shoulder and wailed, and he held me and stroked my hair and said, "Ssh, ssh."

At that moment the unit's token mean nurse, a big white mama with frizzy red hair, came in and saw the two of us in bed together. "Mr. Stewart!" she said. "Get out of her bed immediately!"

"I don't want him to get out of my bed!" I sobbed.

"Look, she's having a hard time here," Nicky said. "I'm just giving her a little comfort."

"I don't care what you're doing," the nurse said. "You need to stop doing it."

"What is wrong with you?" I screamed at her. "Can't you see I'm upset here?"

"I realize you're upset, ma'am, but we can't allow other patients in your bed."

183

"Oh, fudge," I said. And Nicky and I started laughing, and then we were hysterical, and the nurse was furious. She thought we were laughing at her, and not because I'd said "fudge." "Mr. Stewart, I'm giving you five seconds to get out of that bed," she said, and we kept laughing, and finally the nurse just stormed out of the room.

I felt much better after Nicky left. Now I've cooked up a good head of steam. I'm not even angry at Terri. I'm angry at that idiotic shrink in the bin who sat there and stared at me while he smoked his pipe. My parents paid him good money to do nothing but irritate me. After a while I just stopped talking to him. And even then he kept taking their money. What a nerve.

They're sending a shrink in here to talk to me tomorrow. You know what his name is? Dr. Robert Bobb. I'm not kidding. Bob Bobb. His mother must have had quite a sense of humor. It might not be the best idea for him to come in here and try to talk to me with a name like that. With the feisty mood I'm in, I'll be very tempted to ask him about his name. I may even ask him about his mother.

Dr. Robert Bobb came today while Nicky was trying to teach me how to play chess. I don't get chess at all. I've gotten stupider because I'm old and my brain has started to decay. When I was in the bin, some of the ladies had a little bridge club and I asked them to teach me and I picked it up in about fifteen minutes. But now if someone tries to teach me anything I keep having to ask them to repeat everything sixteen thousand times. So Dr. Bobb strolled in just at the moment that I had taken this rook and flung it across the room.

"Woa!" called the shrink. "Looks as though someone is angry." He was a handsome black man with a Jamaican accent.

"She is angry," Nicky said. "She's very angry."

"Are you Dr. Bob Bobb?" I asked.

"I am Dr. Robert Bobb," he replied, in a tone that suggested he was tired of people making jokes about his name.

"Oh," I said. "Well, you might as well sit down. This chess lesson is totally hopeless." I said it without a hint of humor. In fact, I was feeling humiliated about the chess lesson.

"Are you her husband?" Dr. Bobb inquired of Nicky, who had taken his usual Buddha-like position on the bed. "No, I'm not," Nicky said, musically pronouncing the last word in two syllables, which would identify him as a gay man to anyone living in this century. Dr. Bobb may have gotten it because he said, "Oh, a friend, perhaps?"

"Yes, a friend," Nicky said. And then the strangest thing happened. Nicky and Dr. Bobb proceeded to have a conversation about me practically as though I wasn't there. Nicky started to explain what was wrong with me, that I ran into a fire hydrant because I was distraught over this woman who had rejected me, and Dr. Bobb asked me if I thought I needed medication for my depression, and I said no, and Nicky said, as though I hadn't even spoken, "I think she could definitely benefit from some meds." And Dr. Bobb said from all appearances (probably referring to the flying rook) he believed I could benefit from medication as well. Nicky said he was taking Prozac and it saved his life.

"Yes, the SSRI medications are highly effective," Dr. Bobb said. "The only problem is, of course, the sexual side effects."

"I know," Nicky said. "That's part of the reason my boyfriend left me. I just didn't care anymore, you know what I mean?"

"I know exactly what you mean," Dr. Bobb said. "I think it's why my wife left me. Although perhaps a psychiatrist should not be revealing such personal information during a consultation." And he kind of giggled. I was thinking this was the most peculiar conversation I'd ever heard. I was sitting there moving the chess pieces around the board and Nicky said, "Your moves are completely illogical, honey," and I said, "I wasn't trying to make any moves."

"You are just fooling around, am I right?" Dr. Bobb said, smiling, in his lilting accent. I was thinking, Oh my God, I don't even know what planet I'm on. "Seriously, why would your mother name you Robert Bobb?" I asked. "I don't mean to be disrespectful; I'm a journalist and I'm curious about things. Didn't she know that people would call you Bob Bobb?"

"My mother is out of her skull," Dr. Bobb said. "She did it as a joke, so that I would be tormented for the rest of my life."

"Which is why you have to take anti-depressants," Nicky said, and the doctor said "ex-actly," and giggled again. It occurred to me that I may actually have to pay for this ridiculous "consultation." Fortunately, Dr. Bobb did not prolong his visit. He said, "I'm going to prescribe some Zoloft for you. It will help you not care about this woman so much. You will be able to function much better."

"Fine," I said.

"And you make sure she takes it," the doctor said to Nicky.

"Oh, I will," Nicky said. "You can count on it." The two of them smiled at each other like two lovers. I had never seen two men bond with such quick, unbridled enthusiasm. I thought that perhaps I had missed something, since I've become retarded. Dr. Bobb strolled out with his clipboard, and Nicky and I continued with our chess lesson. I didn't dare say anything derogatory about his new lover, Dr. Bobb, because I figured that he would take umbrage. The funny thing was, I kind of liked him too.

October 2000

Well, Dr. Bobb was right. I'm back home and taking Zoloft and now I can function. The day after I left the hospital, Nicky called to let me know that he was going home also, because the doctors had concluded that his headaches were stress-related, and I was highly relieved that he didn't have a brain tumor because after knowing him for two days he'd become one of my best friends. "I don't want to have to come over there and force-feed you," he said, and I could picture him doing that very thing, so I assured him that I would take the Zoloft every day. After I hung up with him, I took the first pill and about four hours later it kicked in and I felt pretty good. I'm not kidding. Everyone said it would take six weeks to work, but I'm a fast metabolizer. Everything I put in my system kicks in very quickly.

So now I get up every morning and relax with a cup of herbal tea and take my pill. I've substituted tea for coffee because coffee throws me into a panic. It's not the savage panic that consumed me before I went on the Zoloft; it's a dull panic, but still not pleasant. So now I'm one of those sissies that I used to make fun of, who drink herbal tea to stay on an even keel and who smile when they're mad.

This Zoloft is great. It makes you not give a shit. If the world ended and you were the only one left, you would look out the window at the smoke and rubble and say to yourself in a flat voice, "How sad. The world is destroyed and I'm the only one left." You would open a can of beans and pick out some books to read. After about two days, you would say, "Hmm. This is kind of a drag to have nobody to talk to." And you would go back to your zombie-like reading.

I love not giving a shit. I SO do not give a shit that I wrote Terri an e-mail, telling her she should not have invited me to her birthday party because it was a royal drag to watch her sitting there making goo-goo eyes at Dee and that she clearly did not appreciate my gift—or *me*, for that matter—and I don't know how I could ever have been so enraptured with her and really don't care if I never see her or speak to her again. After I sent it, I felt triumphant. I didn't know I felt triumphant at first, but a couple hours after I sent it I noticed that the soggy weight in my chest, that had been there ever since that awful birthday party, had lifted. I could breathe easier and my ribs didn't even hurt as much. And I said to myself, "Damn, I'm glad I did that."

Sending that e-mail opened my floodgates. I called Kimba and cried hysterically on the phone for over an hour. I told her how awful it was to realize that I'm a loser and that my life is a big fat nothing and she chastised me for talking that way about myself. She said I wasn't a loser and my life wasn't a big fat nothing, that I'm just going through a bad time, and everyone goes through bad times, and that I'm fun and compassionate and a wonderful friend and I have more strength than most people because I don't compromise. She said I have a lot of integrity. She was so nice and after I hung up with her I felt even better than after I sent the e-mail. So I called a bunch more people. I called my mother and told her that she ruined my life by teaching me to hide my pain and put everyone else's needs before mine, and then I called Willi, who used to be my therapist and is now my friend and told her she was stupid for not figuring out I was gay, and then I called Tommy and told him that I was sick of his derisive attitude and that he was just projecting his own self-hatred onto me and that he was going to die alone in a little room surrounded by beer bottles. The crowning moment was when I called Terri and as soon as she answered the phone I yelled, "Fuck you!" and hung up.

I wonder what people did before Zoloft? Without it, I would just be lying on my bed like a lump. This shit is making me real peppy. Maybe I'll go apply for a job at the White House.

Well, now that this move to DC has proven a spectacular failure, I have decided to make this Godforsaken city my permanent home. A few days ago Gerald, my landlord, told me that the choicest suite in the house was going to be vacated next month. Because I am his most stable tenant (God help him), he offered it to me first. It's a corner suite with two rooms (one small, dumpy one can only be used for storage) and the main room has bay windows and a little balcony overlooking 13th Street. It's freshly painted a pretty lemon yellow, and it has a new carpet, and it will cost three hundred bucks per month more than the little room, but I've gotten a raise, so I can afford it.

I didn't immediately agree to taking the room, because I moved to this city to be with Terri and that's gone down the tubes. But where am I going to go? I'm too demoralized to move to New York City, where I really belong, and forget about moving back to Cleveland. I would die there. So yesterday I told Gerald I would take the place. I'll have to get my furniture moved here from that storage locker in Cleveland, which is the last thing I want to deal with right now. Thinking about it fills me with anxiety. It seems so silly to officially *relocate* here. It's all that bitch Terri's fault. I worked so hard to win her, to have this little slice of happiness, and all I end up with is some nutty friends and a yellow room in a madhouse. I guess it's more than what some people have. But still.

Yesterday Gerald gave me the key to my new place and Kimba and the boys and I broke the place in. We climbed out the window and sat on the balcony and drank beer and watched the traffic on 13th Street, and Johnny and Guillermo passed a joint back and forth. (Jerome neither drank beer nor smoked. He's very particular about his vices.) The boys love Kimba and fawn all over her and she responds with pleasant indifference. "Kimba, maybe you should date Joanna," Guillermo piped up, and Jerome said, "That's what I keep sayin' to Joanna." I said, "Will you guys shut up! Kimba doesn't want to date me," and Kimba smiled and said, "Are you putting words in my mouth again?" I thought that was very cute.

"So when are you moving some furniture into this place?" Jerome asked. I told him my furniture was in a storage locker in Cleveland and that I would arrange to have it moved when I went home for Thanksgiving. "I don't know how I'm going to afford it," I said.

"You can get one of those trucks that moves a lot of people at once," Johnny said. "It's cheaper." He said a friend of his in the moving business could give me more information, and I'm going to call him. But I really didn't want to be talking about the nuts and bolts of my move. I started feeling stressed again.

And then a voice behind us said, "What the hell are you doing out there indulging in vices, you deranged woman?" I looked over my shoulder and there was Nicky in my new room, talking through the open window. I was very excited. I hadn't seen him since I left the hospital. "Get your butt out here and join the party!" I commanded, and he climbed out and I hugged him and introduced him to everyone. He squeezed in between me and Jerome, and I asked him how his headaches were and he said they were a lot better since he stopped thinking so much about "that cad" who left him for another man. But that was as far as our conversation got, because Jerome started whispering little asides into his ear, and soon Nicky was roaring like a schoolboy who'd had too much sugar. Jerome is a genius at seducing highly successful men. He told me he had a lover who was a U.S. Senator and I know it's true. He lies about everything under the sun, but he doesn't lie about stuff like that.

When we all climbed back through the window, Nicky hugged me goodbye, and Jerome left at the same time. I ran to the door and said, "Nicky!" He came back and said, "What is it, sweetie?"

"Use protection," I said.

After everyone left, I actually felt pretty good about Nicky and Jerome. I like my friends to get to know one another, as long as they don't make me feel left out. Not that Nicky and Jerome can include me in all of their, uh, activities. But eventually they'll always come back to mama.

November 2000

It's the day after the election and nobody knows who the *president* is. Isn't that a hoot?

Yesterday I went to Kimba's house for an election night party. She lives in Brookland, a Northeast neighborhood that has a provincial charm and reminds me of Little Italy in Cleveland except it's racially mixed. Kimba invited five women over, including Bette. We sat in Kimba's small living room with its cozy old furniture and sports souvenirs and ate Safeway deli sandwiches and drank beer and watched the returns.

At first the networks reported that Gore was about to win Florida and if that happened he'd have the whole deal pretty well sewn up. So we were all celebrating, dancing around and high-fiving. Even though I'm not exactly enamored with cardboard Al, I was *so* relieved that at least the danger was passing of having that smirking imbecile in the White House right down the street from where I have to shave my legs and brush my teeth. But then, a couple hours later, the networks made *another* hysterical announcement. They said, "Hold everything! We made a mistake! It looks like Al does *not* have Florida in the bag! It seems they are actually neck and neck!" We all started shrieking, "What! What kind of bullshit is *this*?" And then, around 2 a.m., Tom Brokaw said, "We have a final tally in Florida. George Bush has won Florida. George Bush will be the next President of the United States." God. We all just sat there and stared in disbelief. Just imagine having that *cretin* as President of the United States. It would be a disaster. Even people who voted for him for some demented reason, like they are enamored with their gun collections handed down by their great-grandpas or they've seen too many films of fetuses being yanked from uteruses in gooey chunks, even *they* have to admit that should this man become President they would have to play the Scarecrow theme song for him instead of "Hail to the Chief." And anyway I personally cannot stand him. He represents everything I detest. And here were all those media idiots excitedly blathering about Bush getting ready to make his victory speech and Al preparing his concession speech. Everyone went home feeling so dispirited. I went to bed hoping I'd never get up again, because I didn't know how I could endure waking up in a lonely little teeny tiny room with that horrid Dubya as the President-elect.

This morning the phone woke me and it was Kimba. She said, "They're saying the election is now too close to call." I screamed with joy, not only at the news itself, but because a national crisis could take my mind off my stupid nervous breakdown that I've been having for the past two months. Kimba stayed calm, as she always does. She kept making little jokes about Florida, which is the contested state. She said there are some problems with the dimples

202

or the crimples or something in the Florida ballets and they have to recount them. Kimba's twin sister lives in Florida and Kimba has been down there many times and she said they don't know how to do things indoors. She was serious. I haven't laughed that hard in two months.

Actually, everyone in town is laughing. We may not know who the fucking president is for days or even weeks. It will take them that long to figure out who won Florida. I'll bet Bill loves this because he can still be the Big Kahuna in there as long as it lasts. They'll have to drag him out of there, won't they? He's having so much fun being President.

I love Bill. I don't care that he can't keep his weenie tucked in. I think he's adorable. Imagine Dubya addressing the Human Rights Campaign, the national gay advocacy organization, the way Bill did! If he did, he would stumble all over his words and act all uncomfortable and be terrified that one of the men might get within a foot of him and turn him into a queer.

Was that stupid or what—for all those TV networks to announce his victory when he hadn't even won? They make me sick too. They're always trying to call attention to themselves. They think an election is like a spectacular Broadway play with *them* as the narrators and principal characters—kind of like Tom in *The Glass Menagerie*— and they are compelled to say "Good night, Laura, put out your candles," at the end of the night. "Good night, Al, put out your candles." They were afraid they would have to stay up all night and still not have the big news to report, so they just made it up! They wanted to be the big heroes, instead of big nobodies that went home with a goose egg. So they said that Dubya won before he even did. And they really screwed everything up, because now *Al* is the one that has to prove himself because everyone has in mind that *Dubya* won, but they just have to make *sure*.

It probably will be that idiot Dubya. God help us all.

It's Friday after Thanksgiving and I am home for the holiday, in dear little Cleveland. The most extraordinary thing occurred on Wednesday night after Tommy picked me up at the airport. We drove through downtown on the I-71 overpass and the ignited skyline appeared up to our left and I was *enchanted*. Tommy said, "Oh shut up, Werm. It's the same pit stop that it always was." But I saw it differently now that I'm not *stuck* there, like he is. The city looked beautiful. It's a great city on a Great Lake, and I've always thought it does itself a disservice by comparing itself with the behemoths flanking it, New York and Chicago, instead of measuring itself against smaller cities like Toledo or Indianapolis and looking like a winner. There was my exquisite Terminal Tower, and the corporate skyscrapers surrounding it like proud parents (even though they're newer—the child is father to the man), and the radiant embrace of Jacobs Field, and beneath us hissed the wild underbelly that characterizes so many great cities—the industrial flats with its railroad tracks and smokestacks and trash heaps and flotsam and the notorious Cuyahoga River (which once caught on fire and burned the mayor's hair) running through it like healthy bubbling piss. What a glorious town!

I'll be here for a few more days and then I'm going to my storage locker to meet my movers that I hired to transport the rest of my stuff to my new suite at the rooming house. Yesterday at Thanksgiving dinner (which was wonderful—my *meshuggena* family does holidays well), everyone tried to talk me out of it. "Come back to Cleeblands!" my mother beseeched. (She likes to call it "Cleeblands" in honor of the malapropping ballplayer Minnie Minoso.) Dad said in his halting, post-mini-stroke way: "Uh, Joanna, why don't you come back here, do some writing, and get more established, and then make a decision where you ultimately want to live?" (It took him about five minutes to say this, but nobody interrupted him.) Robbie said, "You're just going back there to chase after that woman!" and Micky chimed in with, "Yeah, Jo. You're really making a big mistake." Queen said in her motherly way, "You're going to get hurt again, Peeps."

The only one who made any sense was my older sister, who has not been corrupted by the family system because she didn't enter it until she was forty after I discovered she existed and contacted her, saying it was ridiculous for Dad to have kept her a secret and she should be one of us. Kathleen pounded on the table in her dramatic way (she was once a working actress) and announced, "Listen, you're all full of crap. Joanna made an excellent decision getting the hell out of here and it will do her no good to return and get sucked back into that depressing rut she was in. Furthermore, this city is gray. It has one of the lowest average days of sunlight of all major American cities. Joanna is susceptible to depression and needs to be in a more hospitable climate. I do agree that this woman is poison for her, but she just has to discover that on her own." Then Queen said, "Kathleen is right. Peeps should go back to DC." Mom and Dad just stared at my sisters in disappointment, and my brothers clumped off to watch the game.

But in spite of Kathleen's vote of confidence, I'm feeling depressed about the whole thing. I just let them yammer on about Terri instead of reminding them that it's all over and that she's with someone else. Why are they even still talking about her? They probably think I haven't given up on her. But I have. Then why am I going back there, when my reason for going there is down the tubes and I'm completely out of place among all those people running to meetings in their little suits, and that awful Dubya is going to be my neighbor?

I suppose I'm going back because it's where I *live* now. What am I supposed to do, stay here? That's out of the question. Getting out of here was the best thing I ever did, in spite of all the consequences. I've discovered one of the great ironies, that the way to go back "home" is to get the hell out in the first place. Then you can come back and be enraptured by the skyline and all of a sudden the city becomes part of the stuff you're made of, it enriches you and makes you more complex.

I wonder what DC is doing to the "stuff I'm made of." Maybe it's putting all kinds of crap in it. But if it is, so be it. One thing I can say is that I have no regrets about moving there. No regrets at all.

December 2000

I've been in my new place for two weeks, and on Saturday I had a housewarming party. Bette suggested it. The place didn't feel at all like home when I moved in, the way the little room down the hall did when I first came here. So Bette said that I should invite some people for a "grand opening." I said what the hell, and invited a bunch of people, and they all came, including Karrie, Kimba's twin sister, who was visiting from Florida. Kimba, Karrie, and Bette helped me set everything up. We arranged appetizers from the Safeway on my round coffee table and whipped up a kickin' rum punch, and Kimba got the idea to put a ribbon across the door, to be cut by the first guest, who turned out to be Pia from the potluck group. My friends oohed and aahed at my little apartment, which is rather nice with its French-style bay windows, lemon-yellow walls, new carpet, bookcases, and adornments like my cityscape futon cover, papasan chair, and my brother's paintings covering the walls. We laughed and gossiped and played CDs and danced. Besides Kimba's twin and the potluck group (aka "The Ditches"), my guests included Beanie and Samantha, two of Kimba's friends that I hit it off with at the election party, Johnny and Guillermo, Calliope (who just came for the free food and probably didn't even know whose room she was in), and Jerome and Nicky, who strolled in together. Nicky looked as though he'd just been blasted to the moon in a star-spangled rocket ship, and Jerome looked triumphant. Of course, I'll have to be around to pick up the pieces when Jerome starts depleting Nicky's bank account and cheating on him with men he scoops out of the gutter, but what the hell. That's what friends are for.

I always thought Bette was wilder than Kimba, but it may be the other way around. The two of them did a little ass-bump dance, and it was so burlesque, Kimba's tight little ass shimmying down to meet short Bette's voluptuous ass, and then Bette got tired and sat down and Kimba started yelling at other people to come up and dance with her, and Nicky danced with her for a while, but then everyone was all danced out, so Kimba just kept dancing by herself. She dances like a cowgirl, because she's a country-western dancer. After everyone left and Kimba was helping me clean up (Bette had to go to a benefit), she told me the funniest story about the "dance police" at the lesbian country-western dances she attends, these severe women who two-step according to timeworn rules and accused Kimba of "zigzagging." I said, "So did you stop this zigzagging after they chastised you?" And Kimba said, "Of course not."

Kimba has the cutest smile. It's different from Terri's. Terri has a big grin that stays on her face when she's in a good mood. Kimba smiles almost in spite of herself. When she realizes she's smiling, she stops. I think it's so cute. I don't know what I would do without her. I'm still kind of discombobulated. I kept missing Terri at the party. It didn't feel right that she wasn't there. After everyone left I cried, thinking about the e-mail Terri sent after I called her and said "Fuck you," in which she said she was sorry I was in so much pain and she heard I was in the hospital and hoped I was better, and she wished me "all the happiness you deserve." As nice as the party was, I felt as though it was missing its center. But when I finally settled down in my futon-bed, the last thing I pictured was Kimba and Bette doing that jaunty dance, and when I fell asleep I dreamed about being on a train, clackity-clacking down the road, and wheat fields were all around me, and the Little Rascals were running through the car with that adorable pitbull named Petey. It was a nice dream, far nicer than that awful recurring dream I was having not long ago that I was in hell. It was hell, too. Literally. And I've got news for you, puppies. Hell is *not* hot. It's chilly and damp and looks like a basement. There's even a washing machine down there. Imagine washing your clothes with Adolf Hitler. Wouldn't that be creepy? So you'd better mind your P's and Q's.

Yesterday, the one-year anniversary of my move to DC, I went with Kimba to buy Christmas decorations for her house. We decided to get them in my neighborhood, so I met her at the U Street Metro. I showed up first and waited for about a minute, then she appeared at the bottom of the broken escalator. She stomped up the steps in her blue parka and a Cleveland Browns knit hat, smiling at me the whole way. It wasn't her typical shy, fleeting smile. It was a hell-raising smile, showing her teeth. It was a smile that said, "I'm gettin' ready to kick some butt. How 'bout you, woman?" I was utterly charmed.

The two of us charged through the neighborhood, buying all kinds of stuff. I usually hate shopping, but Kimba is so excited about it that it's infectious. She had me darting around in these old ugly discount stores, yelling, "Look at this!" and "Look at that!" I bought some crazy socks for myself, and then I saw a horrible giant Santa Claus and told Kimba I was going to buy it for her yard, and she hit me on the head with a plastic Jesus. The Latina lady behind the counter saw and was not amused.

After we shopped, Kimba treated me to lunch at Polly's

on U Street to thank me for going with her. When we were waiting for our food, I looked at her and grinned, and she said, "What are you lookin' at?" and I said, "I'm lookin' at you." The girl is adorable. But I'm "not going there," to use the latest pop expression. I've been in too much trouble already.

I went to see Dr. Bobb today in a snow storm. Dr. Bobb is my Jamaican savior even though he's probably clinically insane.

I drove to Dr. Bobb's office in a Zoloft haze. Usually I love driving in a snowfall, but today the flying flakes just thickened the haze. Now that the Zoloft has done its job and I'm no longer hysterical, it's making me feel dead. Driving to Dr. Bobb's, nothing mattered—my friends, my job, my writing. I thought about Kimba and how much fun I have with her and that drew a blank too. Naturally the Howard University Hospital parking lot hadn't been plowed, and I cursed this city that's as incompetent with snow as it is with everything else. One thing about goofy Cleveland, when it snows, they're on it.

Dr. Bobb looked dapper in his winter-white suit and navy shirt and yellow and navy and red tie. He gave me a sunny Jamaican smile, and a little bit of the haze lifted, and I sat down and started screaming about my life. I told him I felt dead, dead, dead. I said that I had been dead my whole life and didn't even know it. I said straight people killed me and put me in deep-freeze, and that they were ignoramuses, thick-skulled morons who think gay people choose to be gay, and that I never would have put up with that idiot Terri's crap if I had any idea how to get over someone, but I never learned because I was deprived of a romantic life because of straight society's sick homophobic tyranny. I continued to rant and Dr. Bobb listened with a little smile on his face.

"I realize now I was *normal* when they put me in a loony bin!" I shrieked. "There was nothing wrong with me. What else do you do when you're fourteen years old with raging hormones and the objects of your affection are *verboten*, except act nutty? Diane Anderson at camp was *verboten*! My cousin Deborah in New York was *verboten*! When I went to visit Deborah and my aunt and uncle in Queens during my summer vacation, my aunt Goldie tried to get me together with this loser next door named Barry Moscowitz that had no friends. His mother used to pick him up from school and take him out to lunch because he had nobody to eat with in the cafeteria. So I should go to the movies with this pathetic Barry Lipshitz instead of going out shopping with my gorgeous cousin, who was five years older and sophisticated and who I adored. I mean, Fuck that. And I did it! That's the kicker! I went to the movies with him and he had terrible B.O., and instead of saying I wanted to leave I sat there and breathed in his stench through the whole damn movie. *I* was protecting *him*! What was wrong with me? And then I didn't even say anything to anyone about his B.O. because I was too nice! Everything all my life was about everyone else but me. Nothing was ever about me!"

217

And Dr. Bobb said, "That's the god's truth, mon. Nothing is ever about you. In this life, the wolves eat the sheep. And when you're young and tender, the wolves can eat you alive."

"But my aunt wasn't a wolf," I said, feeling guilty for complaining about my dead aunt. "She was just trying to show me a good time. She thought it would be nice for me to go out with a boy, even if it was Barry Moscowitz."

"Your aunt was also a sheep, doing the wolves' bidding," said Dr. Bobb. "All those idiots who set the standards for how to live, the sick standards, they are the wolves. We do their bidding while they sit around us and howl."

"Well, they can all go to hell," I said. "They are so clueless. How dare they think that the way *they* are is the only way to be? How dare they rip out my essence and turn me into a sheep? You're right, Dr. Bobb! I was just like one of those wooden sheep in a carnival game, jumping over a fence."

"I as well!" Dr. Bobb said, rearing up in his seat, flame shooting from his eyes. "I was forced to do everything I didn't want to do in Jamaica. I wanted to read, they made me play ball. I wanted to play chess, they made me sell vegetables. The children in my village beat me up every day of my life and my daddy said I deserved it because I was such a sissy. And I wasn't even gay! You know what they told me when I fell for the most beautiful girl in the city? My father and my uncles laughed and said it was like an orangutan trying to catch a butterfly. Well, I caught her all right. And then I was the one who could laugh. I laughed them right out of the deed to our property."

218

"What are you talking about?" I said. "You took their land away?"

"That's right," Dr. Bobb said with a mysterious smile.

"How did you do that?"

"I did it with the use of subterfuge and a very clever attorney. If you look hard enough, you can usually find a loophole to slip into."

"But wasn't it wrong to take their land?" I said.

"No, it wasn't!" he said, slightly popping out of his seat. "You see, Joanna, this is what I try to teach you!" He pointed a finger at me like a charismatic preacher at a tent revival. "This is what I am trying to impress on you! In this life, you have to become a little bit of a wolf."

I told Dr. Bobb the Zoloft had become ineffectual. He said to cut the dose in half and gradually wean myself off. "You're right," he said. "It's better to kick the wall than let the wall kick you."

Whatever the hell that means. I drove home scared out of my mind, realizing that my therapist was a maniac. But then something strange happened. I realized I no longer felt dead. Primal energy oozed through me and a metallic taste of blood eked into my mouth. I thought, "I'll be damned." I howled, "Awooo!" over the steering wheel. And then I howled again. And again. All the way home. And when I walked into the house, I was laughing.

I'm crazier now than when I first came running to DC out of my mind over what's-her-name. I'm offending other lesbians and acting inappropriate with Kimba, and I'm sure the world hasn't seen the worst of it.

Yesterday the potluck group met for a holiday fete at an Adams-Morgan bar, and a few of us were sitting in a conversation nook around a pool table, watching Kimba and another woman play. A beefy, gray-haired woman mentioned that her friend was in Howard University Hospital because of an irregular heartbeat, and I said I had just been there because I had been rejected by this woman and was so upset that I crashed into a fireplug. The beefy woman said, "Well, it's standard procedure to keep you in the hospital after a suicide attempt."

"It wasn't a suicide attempt," I said irritably. "It was carelessness. I was just upset and shouldn't have been driving, and I swerved to avoid a pedestrian and ran into the pole."

Another woman, with a hollow, sunken face, said, "Well, still, they needed to keep an eye on you for a while."

"They needed to keep an eye on me because I had a *concussion!*" I said. "And *broken ribs.* That's why I was in the hospital. Because I had *physical injuries.*"

The two women gave each other knowing looks. I was starting to foam at the mouth but still trying to exercise control. "Why are you guys *looking at each other* like that?" I said. And the gray-haired one said, "We're not guys."

"I am from up north, from the Midwest, and I say 'guys,'" I said. "Where I'm from, 'guys' does not mean 'men.' It's like saying, 'You all.'"

Bette jumped in. "She's right," she said. "You shouldn't take offense at that. It's very hard for northerners to say 'Y'all' or 'you all' for the second person plural. It doesn't come naturally to them.

I said, "Really! What's wrong with 'you guys'? Jesus!" I slammed my drink down on the table and went to the bathroom and kicked the wall, just like Dr. Bobb said I should do. Then I stalked back out and plopped back down on the couch. The hollow-faced woman jerked her eyes back and forth at me like I was a rabid dog and the gray-haired woman said, "Why are you so angry?"

"Why am I angry?" I shouted. "I have a right to be angry! I have recently discovered that my whole damn life has been a sham. I wasted forty years of my life trying to be what other people wanted me to be, and now I have *nothing.* I have no money, no career, no family, no life. The fucking bitch that I loved with my whole heart and soul hasn't the faintest interest in me and I MOVED HERE because of her. I'm going to murder her with an ax! And I happen to know that you two women have equally appalling stories. All gay people do, especially gay people of our generation, because we grew up in a time when who we were, our very essence, was considered equivalent to puke and dirt and scum!" Then I lost my head of steam and got sheepish. I really don't like fighting with people. "Maybe I shouldn't have cut down on my Zoloft," I said to Bette.

Kimba, who was playing pool, said over her shoulder, "No, maybe you shouldn't have."

Bette said, "Oh, please. That's the problem with this whole community. We don't allow ourselves to feel our feelings. I'm sick of it. I grew up in a crazy WASP household with an alcoholic, abusive father and we weren't supposed to talk about it, ever. I spent my whole life learning to express myself honestly and to stop worrying about what everybody thinks. I think you're all being very unfair to Joanna."

"Don't you guys—excuse me, you *all*—ever get pissed off about all the crap you took over being gay?" I asked Gray Hair.

"No," she barked. "My life is my own responsibility and I don't blame other people for my problems."

"Oh, really," I said. "I'll bet you have irritable bowel syndrome."

"Wrong," she said.

"Well, what do you have?" I said. "You must have something."

Kimba turned again after sinking a shot. "Put a lid on it!" she said.

"She needs to get it out," said Bette.

"She needs to stop whining and carrying on," said

Kimba. "This is a holiday party. No one wants to hear it."

"I'll bet she's not as healthy as she claims," I said, ignoring Kimba. "And *she*—" I said, pointing at the hollow-faced one "—*she* probably has—what's that thing everyone has now?" I turned to Bette.

"Fibromyalgia," Bette said.

"Yeah," I said. "Fibromyalgia," I said. "From stuffing everything in."

"You don't get fibromyalgia from that," fumed the hollow-faced woman.

"But you have it, right?"

"Yes, I do have it, and it happens to be caused by environmental toxins."

"Oh, God," I said. I started looking at Kimba's ass as she leaned over the table. "Look at Kimba's ass," I said. "It's cute as hell. Doesn't she have a cute ass, Bette?"

"She does," Bette agreed. "It's adorable."

"You have a cute ass too, honey," I said. "Must be jelly, 'cause jam don't shake like that."

"My mother used to say that!" Bette said.

"So did mine," I said. "That's where I got it."

My two tormenters left, and some other women came in, and before I had a chance to offend them Bette told me to go shoot pool with Kimba, who had taken over the table. Kimba said, "Are you going to behave?"

"I don't like behaving," I said.

Of course, she wiped the table with me. I never shot pool until I became a lesbian and she's been doing it since she was twelve. But since I was drunk I shot a little better than usual. While we were playing, I heard Bette get into a discussion about how ridiculous the whole lesbian community had become. "We used to be angry," she said. "We were separatist. We were conscious of what had been done to us. Now we just eat and listen to Melissa Etheridge and shoot pool and talk about our cats and our mortgages and our stupid jobs. And we're all getting sick, stuffing back our feelings, forgetting what was done to us."

"Oh, brother," Kimba said.

"Look at Kimba's ass," I said again.

I don't remember much of what happened after. Kimba drove me back home on her way home to Brookland and I do remember planting a lip lock on her before leaving the car. Today, when I woke up, I remembered the lip lock. I was kind of embarrassed because Kimba and I are just friends, but so what? I don't care what I do anymore. I'm a wild animal. It's better than being a robot, which is what I was back in the old days.

They think I'm made of money in this damn house.

Yesterday, when I called my bank to check my balance, I discovered I was overdrawn and my checks were bouncing off the wall. When I asked the representative to go over my charges he found one for $216 from Enterprise Car Rental, which I never authorized.

I screamed about the thieves at Enterprise Car Rental and then I hung up in a huff. It made no sense. Last week Jerome came in here followed by Johnny and Guillermo and one of their thug friends, and he asked me if I could rent a car for them for one day, using my credit card. He said they would pay me in cash. I said no, no, no, and finally I caved in, knowing he would just nag me until I fell over dead. I drove the four of them to the rental place on K Street and paid for a one-day rental and they sneaked off in the car (since I was supposed to be the driver) and I went home.

After I got off the phone with the bank yesterday, I marched into Guillermo's room and found him lying on his bed with the thug that had been with them that day. "Why did Enterprise Car Rental charge me an extra two hundred and sixteen dollars?" I demanded, waving my checkbook at them. "I'm overdrawn and my checks are bouncing and I am *very upset!*"

"Oh, honey, I'm so sorry," Guillermo said. "Jerome said he'd take care of it."

"What do you mean, Jerome said he'd take care of it? Take care of what?"

"We kept the car for two extra days," Guillermo said.

I couldn't believe this. "What's the matter with all of you?" I yelled. "How could you do that? Do you think I'm rich? You guys owe me two hundred and ninety-eight dollars, which includes exorbitant charges for three bounced checks! Who's going to give me that money? If I don't get it, Gerald's going to kick me out of here because I won't be able to pay the rent! Has that occurred to any of you lunatics?"

"See?" Guillermo said to his friend. "I told you we shouldn't keep the car." He turned to me. "Joanna, I swear. I told Jerome, 'We can't fuck up Joanna.' And he swore to us that he would take care of it. Didn't he, Petey?"

"Yeah, he did," said Petey. "He swore."

"Why did you believe him? You know how he is. And anyway, what were you all doing driving around in a rental car for three days? Delivering laundry? I don't get this."

"We were cruising," Guillermo said. "Jerome picked up this guy that was dreamy, Joanna." He smiled beatifically.

"I don't know why you had to go cruising at my expense. Did Nicky know Jerome was tooling around snatching men out of alleys?"

"Oh, it didn't mean nothing," Guillermo said. "We

226

were just having fun. Nicky is Jerome's heart. You know that."

"Well, I suppose I have to talk to Mr. Big," I said, and went down the hall to Jerome's room. He wasn't in there, but the window was ajar and I looked out and saw footsteps in the melting snow on the fire escape. Jerome must have been listening to our conversation and escaped out the window. I returned to my room and called Nicky and told him what happened. "That bastard was cheating on me?" Nicky said. I rolled my eyes, more concerned at the moment about my $298, although I did feel a little bad for Nicky. I listened to him carry on about Jerome's "despicable behavior" and then I had to go to work.

When I got home, I found an envelope under my door with a check for $298, signed, of course, by Nicky. I went into Jerome's room and found him unperturbed by the whole fiasco. "Why did you make Nicky pay for your . . . indiscretions?" I said. "That's not right!"

Stretched out on his bed, Jerome looked at me through half-lidded eyes. "Don't worry about it, Sweet Meat," he drawled. "He'll get his money back. Trust me. Do you think I would do anything to hurt my one true love?"

Tonight is New Year's Eve.

A couple days ago I got a coupon in the mail for a New Year's Eve party at Colonel Brooks Tavern, an Irish-style tavern in Kimba's neighborhood known for its conviviality and excellent food. I thought it would be the perfect thing for me and Kimba to do, especially since it's two blocks from her house and we wouldn't have to drink and drive.

I called Kimba and got her machine, and it occurred to me that I hadn't heard from her in two days. Just as I was hanging up the phone, Jerome appeared in my doorway. He stood there with his arms folded and a proprietary look on his face and said, "Do you know where your girlfriend and my boyfriend are?"

"I don't have a girlfriend," I said.

"Yes, you do. And your girlfriend, Kimba, and my boyfriend, Nicholas, happen to be on a romantic weekend in Berkeley Springs, West Virginia, getting massages and lying naked in the hot springs."

I felt vaguely annoyed that I didn't know anything about this. "What are you talking about?" I said. "Where did you hear this?"

"I just got a call from Nicky," Jerome said. "Trust me. They are both naked, as we speak."

This should have been funny, but for some reason I was irritated. Kimba was always flying around in her own orbit, not telling people what she was doing. And Nicky was *my* friend, not hers. "I can't believe Kimba didn't tell me about this," I said. "What *is* this? Since when did Kimba and Nicky become bosom buddies?"

"Don't ask me," Jerome said. "Sounds like they're *real* bosom buddies now. If you catch my drift."

I had to laugh at this. "That's the craziest thing I ever heard," I said. "Maybe they're naked, but they're not fucking. Nicky is a fairy. Kimba is a dyke. Hello."

"That don't matter," Jerome said. This scared me. When it comes to sexual matters, Jerome is unassailable.

"You think they're *fucking* in Berkeley Springs?" I said.

"That's what Nicky implied," said Jerome. "He said he'd only been with a woman once and Kimba is more woman than anyone he'd ever known and her naked body reminded him of a wild leopard."

"He's just trying to make you jealous!" I said. "You think you can keep fucking one man after another without Nicky getting upset about it?"

"That's just business," Jerome said coolly. I snorted and he said speaking of business he had to tend to some and he left.

Yesterday Kimba called me and asked me if I wanted to go to a poetry reading at Politics and Prose, the leftie independent bookstore on Connecticut Avenue.

"Where were you this weekend?" I said.

"Berkeley Springs," Kimba said.

229

"With Nicky?" I asked.

"Yes," Kimba said in a smug little voice, as though to say, "So what?"

"God, Kimba," I said. "You and Nicky just run off to Berkeley Springs? I didn't even know you guys had become such good buddies. It's peculiar that I wouldn't even know about this!"

"You don't have to know everything," Kimba said. I rolled my eyes.Then she placated me with an explanation. "We had made plans to go to the big flea market in Harper's Ferry and then we decided to make a weekend of it," she said.

I still couldn't understand why no one told me. I like to be in on everything. I was suddenly afraid to ask Kimba if she wanted to go to Colonel Brooks Tavern for New Year's Eve.

"Listen, I got this coupon for a New Year's Eve party at Colonel Brooks Tavern," I said. "I thought you and I could go."

"Okay," Kimba said.

"Do you want to invite Nicky?" I asked. I thought maybe she couldn't get along without her new best friend.

"Fine," Kimba said inscrutably. I couldn't tell if she wanted to invite Nicky or not. She drives me nuts sometime. I grew up around Jews who spew out their thoughts as they're occurring, and Kimba doesn't speak her thoughts until after she's processed and organized them, and not even then sometimes. I get nervous when I can't tell what someone's thinking.

But Kimba didn't hesitate to express herself when I asked if we should invite Jerome. "No!" she yelled. And I realized that Nicky and Kimba had probably plotted their weekend excursion to fuck with Jerome's head.

"Jerome said you two were having a romantic naked weekend together," I said.

"I told Nicky to call him on his cell phone while we were naked in the hot springs," Kimba said in her innocent little voice that I knew was accompanied by an evil smile.

"So you two *were* naked in the hot springs."

"Yes, but obviously we weren't fucking." I felt very foolish for letting Jerome put disorienting thoughts in my head.

Nicky told me he would love to celebrate New Year's Eve with me and Kimba. I felt a little bad about excluding Jerome, but Nicky said, "If you invite that son-of-a-bitch, I'll kill you," and then he came over and (as he told me later) stormed into Jerome's room, threw Jerome's bracelet back in his face, and said he was sick and tired of being one of "literally hundreds of men" and being "extorted every time I turn around." He concluded by declaring that he never wanted to see Jerome again as long as he lived. So I guess that took care of that.

I'd better stop writing and figure out what to wear tonight. I know. I'll wear my brown velvet jeans and my silk multicolored shirt that I've had since the eighties. The shirt is so retro it's cool. Not that Kimba will notice. She thinks compliments are gushy. Of course, the flip side of it is, when she gives you one you know she means it.

January 2001

I have no idea what to make of our New Year's Eve get-together. All I know is that it was a hell of a lot better than last year's, when I sat in my room alone with a champagne bottle that I couldn't open, pining for Mrs. Satan.

Unlike last year's balmy night, Friday it was snowing like crazy, and I felt kind of lonely traveling to Kimba's on the Metro through the winter night. But my loneliness vanished as soon as I walked in the house and laid eyes on my friend, all decked out in black velvet pants and a green silk shirt and a black vest. Her freshly colored hair was bright and rakish, and she wore dangling silver earrings, which tickled me.

Kimba said she just got off the phone with Nicky and he was changing trains and would meet us at the tavern. "I don't know what kind of mood he'll be in," she said. "He just had another fight with Jerome." She said Jerome was reneging on his promise to move in with him.

"*What?*" I shrieked. "Nicky said he just *broke up* with him!" Kimba gave me a sidelong look that said everything, and I laughed dolefully. "God," I said. "He'll rob

Nicky blind and give him AIDS and who knows what else. The man has lost his mind."

"Tell *him*," Kimba said, grabbing her bomber jacket.

We walked easily though the snowstorm, two Northeast Ohio girls feeling superior to all the Southerners who were intimidated by snow. We got to the tavern, a big, clean, old place with polished wood floors and tables, and it was full but not crowded. They put us in a booth where we had a direct view of the huge, tastefully decorated Christmas tree. (I'm one of those Jews who appreciates Christmas trees, unlike some of my compatriots who hate them because as children they felt left out of winter holidays, which makes no sense to me because we had Chanukah, and anyway it's creepy to begrudge gentiles their seasonal joy.)

Kimba and I ordered whisky sours, which was my idea because it seemed appropriate for an Irish-style bar. Just as the drinks arrived, Nicky walked in. He wore a wool coat over jeans and a brocaded vest, and he looked handsome. He shook the snow off, hung up his coat, and then kissed us both and sat down next to Kimba. He put his arm around her and she smiled a mysterious smile, and I thought, "Maybe Jerome was right about them." But Nicky removed his arm right away.

"What can I get you, sir?" asked the waiter.

"Scotch on the rocks, said Nicky.

"Any particular kind?"

"I don't care," said Nicky. "Just something decent." He settled into a comfortable slouch and said, "I'm not going to rant and rave about the asshole. I won't. This is New Year's Eve."

236

But then he did. He said he was hopelessly in love with Jerome, who did not deserve his love. "He's not even human," said Nicky. "He's an animal. I mean literally. Which makes me guilty of bestiality."

"Jerome is a beast," I said. "Have you checked his scalp? I'm sure he has six-six-six pigmented on there."

"I don't have to check his scalp," Nicky said. "It's there. Undoubtedly, it's there."

"You're just in love with the sex," I said. "I know the man is a sex machine, and he could make a piece of granite come."

Nicky's face slackened into a silly smile. "Oh, honey," he said. "You have no idea."

"Jesus," I said.

"It's not just that," Nicky said. "He has more raw charm than anyone I know. I took him to my office party, and he schmoozed up those attorneys as though they were clay in his hands. He cornered this heterosexual judge and fifteen minutes later the judge was laughing like a little boy at Jerome's jokes and his wife was standing next to him, looking annoyed."

"He reminds me of Ted Bundy," Kimba said.

"Honey, that man makes Ted Bundy look like Jeffrey Dahmer," Nicky said.

At that moment, Jerome sashayed in, covered with snow. He wasn't even wearing a coat. He had on brown corduroy pants and timberland boots and a yellow shirt and a yellow scarf, and he looked like John Shaft. My first thought was that Kimba would leave.

"Hello, ladies," Jerome said, grinning.

"What are you doing here?" Nicky said coldly. Jerome

slid in the booth next to me and said to Nicky, "Hello, darling." Nicky's face softened, and then he turned to Kimba, his next victim. "Hello, Kimba, my love," he said. "I brought you something." He took a small box out of his pocket and pushed it across the table. "What is it?" Kimba said. Ordinarily she would be suspicious, but after a potent whisky sour she had kind of a dopey smile on her face. Jerome had probably waited until he knew we would be inebriated before descending on us.

"Open it and see," he said.

Inside the box was a stunning grasshopper pin, with a tiny diamond between the wings. "Only the best for the best," Jerome said in his buttery baritone. Kimba stared at it.

"What did you do, steal it from one of your whores?" snapped Nicky.

"No, I didn't steal it," replied Jerome. "My sister gave it to me. It was my mother's. I went to my sister's in Virginia last week and I saw it in her room. I remembered that Kimba liked grasshoppers, so I told my sister my mother promised that pin to me and she gave it to me." Most likely his mother had promised no such thing.

Kimba smiled at the grasshopper, then she took it out and pinned it on her vest. It looked beautiful. The way to her heart is through *stuff*. She collects colored glass and sports memorabilia and bears, but her passion is grasshoppers, because her first toy was a stuffed grasshopper. "Thank you," she said to Jerome. "That was sweet."

Nicky sneered. "You are so shameless," he said to Jerome, and Jerome smiled proudly.

And then we proceeded to have the most marvelous

time. Jerome told Nicky he had put a down payment on a large-screen TV for them, and Nicky said, "What makes you think I want to cohabitate with you after all the shit you put me through?" and Jerome said, "It's mutual." Kimba said, "Nicky never put you through any shit," and Jerome said, "Kimba, you don't know. He plays with my heart like it's a toy mouse." Of course, that was a lie too, but it made Nicky smile, thinking that maybe he had some power in this relationship after all.

After we ate some appetizers and were midway through our third drinks, Kimba leaned across the table and said to me, "You look radiant tonight. Why don't you ever wear that shirt?"

"I was saving it for a special occasion," I said. Kimba had this look on her face, and even though I knew it was from the whiskey it was delightful. It made me feel good. It occurred to me later that I didn't think about Terri once the whole night. We were having too much fun. Jerome got into a conversation with the straight couple next to us, and we all ended up laughing hysterically about the absurdity of human body parts, like fingers and toes, and then we got into how funny noses were. We were even laughing too loud for the rest of the people in the bar, who were looking at us askance. It reminded me of my family in a restaurant, being noisier than everyone else.

When midnight approached, we stood up with our champagne glasses except Jerome, who sat at the table like the family patriarch, drinking his club soda and lime. When the ball went down, the straight couple kissed and Nicky kissed Jerome and Kimba kissed me and it wasn't a "friend" kiss. Then I kissed Nicky and Kimba kissed Nicky and I kissed Jerome on the cheek and he sat there looking very pleased with himself, after having accomplished his mission of winning us over. We capped off the ceremony with Nicky and me hugging the straight couple.

Nicky and Jerome went off into the flying snow and Kimba and I walked home, holding hands. Usually I sleep in her guest room, but she invited me into her room. Once we were in bed we started kissing, and laughing, and kissing, and laughing. I pulled up her silky white undershirt and licked her one nipple, and then we rolled around and kissed some more. Then we started talking about those two irritating women at the Adams-Morgan bar, and Kimba made this face, imitating the gray-haired woman, that totally cracks me up. I started singing, "If I Were A Rich Man," because her favorite movie is *Fiddler on the Roof*, and she joined in, and I taught her the Yiddish word "klepkeh," an angry thought that gets stuck in your head. She said, "Is Lucille a klepkeh?" referring to her boss, and I said, "No, no. A person can't be a klepkeh." But that cracked me up too. We didn't go all the way, but that was fine. We fell asleep with my arm curled around her.

In the morning Kimba made us a big fluffy-egg-and-bacon breakfast, with coffee for me and tea for her. I didn't have a hangover, and I wondered why. I always feel pain after a night of heavy drinking. The only time I didn't was after spending a night with Terri. That makes me think maybe I'm falling for Kimba, but I can't be, because I don't feel at all about Kimba the way I felt about Terri. It's just that she's my first really close, intimate friend

240

since I came out, so it's kind of like she's been with me since I was born. I have the kind of love for her that you have for a girlhood friend. When she called me yesterday and said how much fun she had, I kind of melted. I can't explain it.

Everything is a big mess now. Terri called about an hour ago and everything I have accomplished over the past three months is in tatters. She called to inform me that things are not working out between her and Dee. She said Dee is superficial and boring.

"I didn't get the impression that Dee was superficial and boring," I said. "I thought she was charming and intelligent." I couldn't believe how disgusting Terri was, trashing someone's entire personality just out of spite, and at the same time I was ecstatic that Terri was getting rid of Dee. In fact, as soon as I heard her voice—"Knadel?"—I almost swooned. I couldn't help it. I think the woman's done something unalterable to me.

"She has some minor redeeming qualities," Terri said.

"Like what?"

"To tell the truth, I can't think of any at the moment," Terri said. "They're inconsequential."

"I suppose you think Dee Williams is completely devoid of any positive qualities because you behaved like a selfish bitch with her and she got sick of it," I said.

"That is unfair," Terri said, sounding amused. She loves it when I tell her off.

"Well, are you done with her or what?" I said.

"We're going to have a talk on Friday. But as of now we're not seeing each other." She told me that last weekend the two of them went to a resort in the Shenandoah Valley and it did not go well. Every time Terri travels with a woman, it doesn't go well. She has to do everything her way, and if the other person wants to do something else, she becomes furious.

"What happened?" I asked.

"She was two hours late, and you know I hate to be late," Terri said. "On Saturday, she wanted to go on a hike through the mountains when it was 10°. I told her to go ahead, but she wouldn't. She just stayed in the room and sulked. And then I wanted to have the five-course meal at the resort and she wanted to drag me to a barbecue shack out in the boondocks that her relatives told her about."

I had to concede that a barbecue shack was not the best choice for a vegetarian. "What did she expect you to eat at this barbecue shack?" I asked.

"I don't know, Knadel."

"Well, it's strange that she would want to drag you to some barbecue shack that had no vegetarian food," I said, suspecting there was more to the story. "But I can't blame her for not wanting to go on some hike through the mountains all by herself."

"It was 10°, honey," Terri said.

I started to get irritated with the whole conversation. Why am I discussing Terri's relationship with her, I thought. This has nothing to do with me. But I couldn't stop. "I suppose you refused to have sex with her, after she did all the wrong things," I said.

"True," Terri said. "I didn't feel like it."

I had lifted off into this ridiculous euphoric state and was tumbling through the air like a stunt plane with Buddy Hackett at the controls, like in the movie *It's a Mad, Mad, Mad, Mad World*. I needed to get a grip. I needed to get off the phone and call Dr. Bobb, or Kimba, or Bette, or my mom, or someone who could ground me.

"Well, if Dee Williams is such a loser, then just tell her on Friday that you're done," I said.

"I think that's where it's going," Terri said.

"All right, Bumble Bee," I said. "Let me know what happens." Immediately I screamed at myself, "Why are you call-ing her an endearment, Joanna? What's the matter with you?"

As soon as I hung up, the phone rang and it was Kimba. I told her what had just happened and she said, "What are you going to do when they break up?"

"What do you mean?" I said. "Do you think they will?"

"Of course they will."

"Well, what do you mean, what am I going to do?"

"How do you feel about Terri and Dee breaking up?"

"Well, I'm not exactly heartbroken. I mean. You know."

"Well, then," Kimba said. "You just have to bide your time."

"Oh fuck her," I said. "She's dead meat. I'm done with her."

"No, you're not," Kimba said in a tiny little voice. "You're not done with her at all." I heard her cell phone ring and she said, "Gotta go," and hung up.

244

I called Dr. Bobb. "Come in right now," he said. "I am not talking about leaving in five minutes. I am talking about hanging up the phone, picking up your keys, walking out the door, and driving to my office. I will expect you here in fifteen minutes."

That was a half hour ago, but instead of immediately going to Dr. Bobb's office I decided to write this. I need to process Terri's call so I can contend with Dr. Bobb, who will try to impose some mandate on me. But writing this isn't doing any good because I still feel like that crazy Buddy Hackett in the stunt plane, and I'm worried that Kimba is angry at me, and goddammit, there's the phone. I'm sure it's him. I'd better go see him before he sends one of those psychiatric ambulances out here to fetch me. It will ruin my whole reputation around here.

Dr. Bobb was waiting for me with a toy top, one of those things you spin around and around and it floats into the air and then settles back down into the base. When I walked in, I saw the top float up and hover, and Dr. Bobb looked at me and smiled. "Come on in!" he said, standing up. "How do you like my toy?"

"It's cool," I said. "I haven't seen one of those things since I was a kid."

"That's how long I've had it," he said.

"Does it have some significance?" I said. The hovering top seemed suspiciously metaphoric.

"Everything has significance," Dr. Bobb smiled. "Would you like to try?"

I spun the top in its base and it flew up and actually hit the ceiling. Dr. Bobb cracked up. He leaned back in his leather chair and laughed until tears came. "I've seen you hit the ceiling before, Joanna, but not quite like that," he said between gasps of laughter. "The man is crazy," I thought. I sat down on his love seat. "Let's try again," Dr. Bobb said, and started playing around with the top again.

"What's *wrong* with you?" I said. "Why are you playing around with that top? I'm losing my marbles here and you're playing with a top."

"We're waiting for someone," Dr. Bobb said.

"Who?" I said. "I don't want to see anyone. It's not Terri, is it? Did you call Terri?" I leapt halfway out of the sofa.

"Relax," Dr. Bobb said. "I don't even know Terri's number."

"Well, who is it, then?"

Dr. Bobb picked up the base of his top and examined it. "Hmm," he said. "Interesting aerodynamics."

I heard the elevator open, and two seconds later in walked Nicky. "I got here as soon as I could, Dr. Bobb," he said, with this "emergency response" look on his face.

"Oh, for God's sake," I said. "What is *wrong* with you two?"

"Nothing is wrong, Joanna," Dr. Bobb said. He and Nicky hugged. "How have you been?" Dr. Bobb asked, his eyes gleaming.

"Uh," Nicky waved. "You don't want to know."

"Yes, you don't want to know," I said. "The person you have summoned to restore my sanity has fallen in love with a sociopath who cheats on him with a different man every day, extorts money from him, and thinks safe sex is a quaint notion invented by silly alarmists."

Nicky fell into the love seat next to me. "She's right," he said.

"Nicky!" Dr. Bobb said. "This is true?"

"It's true, Dr. Bobb," Nicky moaned. "But the man is a sexual Svengali. I am helpless in his spell."

"Well, it seems to me that you both need a severe beating," Dr. Bobb said.

"We do, we do," Nicky said. He turned to me. "So I understand you got a call from the evil bitch," he said.

"She's not an evil bitch," I said, feeling a bit protective of my first love.

"She is an evil bitch with you!" Dr. Bobb yelled. Suddenly he was standing in front of me, looming over me like a scary high school principal. "She is trying to lure you back into her den so she can devour you in chunks. Do not let it happen!" I stared at him. He returned to his desk and sat down. He pushed aside his top, folded his hands, and looked at me. "You are going to check in with Nicky twice a day," he said. "You are going to focus on the positive things in your life."

"Really," Nicky said. "She has this woman who loves her like crazy, and this woman is as precious as gold, and she treats her like an old shoe."

"You are talking about Kimba?" Dr. Bobb said.

"What are you talking about?" I screamed. "Kimba is a good, dear friend! Well, maybe I have a little bit of a crush on her, but we're still *friends*! It's perfectly normal to like your friend and maybe even fool around with her a little. So what? We're *very dear friends*. What's the matter with you people anyway?"

"See?" Nicky said to Dr. Bobb. And Dr. Bobb said, "Yes, I see."

"Both of you are crazy!" I yelled. "You don't ..."

"All right, mon!" Dr. Bobb said, waving his hands in front of me. "Let's focus on a less threatening positive in your life. Your writing. What are you writing these days, besides that diary that's exacerbating your neurotic self-involvement?"

"Nothing," I said.

"I want you to write another article for the *City Rag*," Dr. Bobb said. "This will boost your self-confidence. Terri turns you into a wimp. The antidote to that is writing. Writing strengthens you. It gets the juice flowing through your body. Good, healthy juice. Not toxic juice laced with the chemical equivalent of cocaine."

The man is an odd kind of genius. He scored a bull's-eye with the writing suggestion. I had been thinking that I was overdue for a second article. People were forgetting all about my piece on gentrification.

"Okay," I said. "I'll submit some ideas to the editor."

"Good, good. When will this happen?"

"Tomorrow," I said. I meant it, too.

"All right, then. Don't wait till the day after tomorrow." Dr. Bobb turned his attention to Nicky. "And you, my friend, also require intervention," he said. Nicky squirmed. "Is this lover boy of yours HIV positive?"

"Yes," Nicky said. "But believe me, Dr. Bobb, I am very careful. I may be emotionally unstable, but I'm not suicidal."

"Well, okay, then," Dr. Bobb said. "I'm happy to know that. But besides that, is Joanna's characterization of him accurate? Is he a sociopath?"

"Yes," Nicky said. "But what she didn't tell you, Dr. Bobb, is that he's her friend! *She* introduced me to him! He lives in her building and she spoils him rotten, more than I do!"

"Tsk, tsk, tsk," Dr. Bobb clucked, shaking his head. "This is bad."

"Well, he is kind of my friend," I said. "He lives right

on my floor, so we've become friendly. But I never encouraged Nicky to get together with him. It was a total accident. Nicky came to visit one day and Jerome was there and he started flirting with him, and it was like a fluff ball being sucked up into a tornado. What was I supposed to do?"

"You pull the fluff ball out of the tornado. Like this." Dr. Bobb grabbed his top, sent it into the air, and then grabbed it and slammed it back into the base. I'm surprised the thing didn't break. "Sometimes you have to push against gravity," he said. He got up out of his chair. "Now get the hell out of here," he said. "Both of you. I want to see you back here on Monday, Joanna."

"What about Nicky?" I said. "All I did was answer the phone when Terri called. Nicky is actually in a *relationship* with a destructive force."

"Nicky has his own therapist," Dr. Bobb said. He looked at Nicky. "Am I right?" he said. "Aren't you seeing my colleague, Dr. Jordan?"

"No, I am not," Nicky said. "I quit him after two sessions. Dr. Jordan has the I.Q. of a fish."

"Nicky!" Dr. Bobb said. "You need to be seeing someone! I know what you mean about Dr. Jordan. I will refer you do someone else." He started writing on a piece of paper.

"Why can't he see you?" I asked Dr. Bobb.

"Because we are friends, like you and Kimba," Dr. Bobb said. "You cannot see your friend in therapy." He smiled at Nicky and Nicky smiled back, the way they had in the hospital the first time they met. I never saw anything like it. They were besotted with each other. I

250

wanted to make a funny comment, but I was speechless. Together they constitute a force that defies commentary.

When I got home, I realized I hadn't really thought about Terri since I walked into Dr. Bobb's office. Dr. Bobb and Nicky had cleverly distracted me from her. But not thinking about her isn't the same as not *feeling* her. I'm still hovering nauseously in the air. And Bob Bobb can talk all he wants about defying gravity, but it's kind of hard to slam yourself down into your base.

February 2001

This house is turning into a slum.

The respectable people have moved out and street people moved in. Courtly Tomas moved back to Brazil and two baggy-pants thugs moved into his room with a girl that I can tell is a crackhead. The two thugs have already come into my place, pretending to introduce themselves as my new neighbors, but they were just casing my room and now I need to get a double lock. The three of them hang out in Jerome's room with that horrid Calliope and I hear them all shrieking "mother-fucker" this and "motherfucker" that except for Jerome, who doesn't curse. Meanwhile Donald got disgusted and left after Ginger and Calliope stole his credit card once too often, and two white druggie-looking sisters moved into his room and whenever I pass them in the hall they give me that eerie look that junkies give you before they get up the nerve to hit you up for money. This afternoon, I saw the two of them hanging out in the hall with the three other charming newcomers, probably plotting with them how to rip people off. They ignored me until I passed and then I know they were looking at me.

The place has gotten filthy. Russell, the manager, used
to keep it spotless, but about a month ago Gerald fired
him because (according to Russell) he spurned Gerald's
advances and Gerald got huffy and said, "Don't come
back tomorrow." So now the carpeted floors are filthy and
littered with cigarette butts and the kitchen is solid
grease and the living room smells like a zoo and, in fact,
the whole place smells like a zoo except for my place
which I deodorize with plug-in devices that are probably
giving me cancer.

Tommy wanted to visit and I put him off because it
has turned into the flophouse that he warned me about
and I can't have him come here and see it. I don't want to
have my girlfriends over here anymore, although Bette
has been here and seems amused by the whole scene. I'm
afraid to tell Kimba what's been happening because she's
been acting distant since Terri called and I'm afraid she'll
say she won't ever come over here again.

Thank God for Johnny and Guillermo. They're still
my buddies, and they give me comfort. They hang around
with thugs too, but their thuggish Latino buddies are
benign compared to the two thugs who moved in here,
who have that dangerous look. And the worst thing is
that Jerome has become their guru. The thugs and the
crackhead go into his room and gather around him while
he watches TV and feeds them that slop from Yum's. I
don't understand Jerome. He may be a sociopath, but he's
also a very bright man. What does he see in them?

Now I'm a monster in the lesbian community because I took Dr. Bobb's advice and wrote another piece for the *City Rag*. It was a funny essay about the play party Terri and I attended last summer, but a lot of lesbos around here don't appreciate my humor.

Without using any identifying information, I wrote about the innocuous "dominatrix" squirting fluid up someone's pussy, and the whipping scene with the bored-looking women, and the anxious guests wandering around in their leather and cop uniforms and the absence of any kind of rebellious mood. I concluded by saying it was a "sorry day" when the S&M contingent of the lesbian community threw a party that had all the electricity of a junior high school dance.

It was meant to be tongue-in-cheek, but apparently nobody got it because the following week the paper was full of letters from dykes all over town, spewing vitriol. If you ask me, the letters confirmed my underlying point—that lesbians around here are terrified of appearing too wild or rebellious and prefer to blend into the mainstream. "For Ms. Kane to imply that this sorry carnival represents our

community is outrageous," wrote an officer of the largest
national gay advocacy group in the nation. (I never implied any such thing.) "Sadomasochism is not a custom in
our community," wrote another goody-two-shoes. "It is
an aberration." Another woman wrote that the women
were acting out abuse traumas of their childhoods and for
me to be ridiculing them was "true sadism." God. Don't
they have a sense of humor around here?

To make things worse, I've gotten little support on the
home front. Bette loved my essay and Nicky and Jerome
chortled over it, but that was about it. Kimba didn't even
bother to call me, and after I called her and asked her
what she thought she said she liked my piece but then
she abruptly changed the subject, telling me about plans
she made with people I didn't even know. Worst of all,
yesterday I got this repugnant e-mail from Terri which
said, "Good writing, but I'm not sure it was appropriate
for *City Rag. The Washington Blade,* perhaps?" I wanted to
kill her. The whole point was to make the straight world
aware of us, not write something about lesbians and hide
it away in the damn *gay Blade.* Since Terri was *with* me at
that ridiculous party, I was hoping that she would be
amused by my piece, but no! She just *had* to diss it. I hate
her with a boiling passion.

I know I'm taking out on Terri all my hurt over those
angry letters and Kimba acting so strange. But I can't
help it. I'm back to obsessing about her, but now it's in a
rageful way. I wish she never sent me that e-mail, but if
she didn't say *anything* I would be just as furious. Everyone's sick of hearing it. Bette said, "You knew what she
was going to say," and Tommy said I've gone back to

being a Sputnik circling around her and my sister Queen said I should forget about Terri and concentrate on Kimba, and when I told her Kimba wasn't being very nice she said, "There's probably a good reason for it."

The most disconcerting reprimand was from Nicky, who said if I couldn't stop carrying on about Terri Dr. Bobb would employ some kind of de-programming technique on me that the two of them discussed. As it turns out, Nicky is seeing Dr. Bobb in therapy, in spite of their unnatural attraction to each other. I'm sure they just sit around and discuss how fucked up everyone is with the exception of them. So now they're plotting to inflict some kind of radical treatment on me just because I'm justifiably upset over no one appreciating my essay.

Maybe I should agree to the treatment. I could end up having the sublime S&M experience that creepy party failed to provide. On second thought, with Dr. Bobb at the controls it could get out of hand. What if he turns me into a salmon or a hamster? I'd better be careful about what I say around Nicky for a while.

Dee broke up with Terri and asked me out, which is wonderful because now I can get back at Missy for trying to destroy me. Also it will be a good distraction from being upset over Kimba, who never even calls anymore and acts like an insolent teenager when I call her. I'm afraid to ask her what's going on because her response might not be nice and I'm too vulnerable to hear it right now. I hate to say it, but men are a lot easier to deal with than women. You always know what they're thinking.

When the phone rang yesterday, a silky voice said, "Joanna?" and when I confirmed my identity, Dee didn't even say who it was, which I thought was cute, that she assumed I knew. She just said, "I loved your piece in the *City Rag.*" She said she laughed all the way through it, and that she agrees with me that our community could use a little more flavor. She said other places she'd lived, like Colorado and California, had real kick-ass lesbians that strutted around in ragged denim vests and spikey hair. "I'm talking about women in their fifties and sixties," she said. "I never went to their sex parties, but I'm sure they were spicier than this one." I mentioned that Terri had

260

been with me at the party and she knew this, and then she said that she and Terri had broken up.

Dee said she got sick of Terri's selfishness. The turning point was their "romantic getaway" in the Shenandoah Valley. She said Terri was sullen and uncooperative and ruined the whole weekend. I said I'd talked to Terri and mentioned the barbecue shack that Dee wanted to drag her to even though she's a vegetarian, and Dee laughed her musical laugh and she, "What a jerk! Did she tell you the reason I wanted to take her there?" She said the place was known for its mock barbecue, and was a *favorite* of vegetarians, and Dee had been talking to Terri about it for weeks and was planning the whole trip around it, and then Terri refused to go just to be spiteful. That was so typical of Terri I laughed and laughed. I assumed this was after Terri had become disenchanted with Dee, because when she's wooing someone she's all "gentlemanly," but after she becomes disenchanted she's like Idi Amin.

Dee asked me if I wanted to go with her to La Rouche, a French bistro in Georgetown. She said she knew my birthday is coming up (how did she know?) and dinner was on her. Of course I said yes. I've always liked Dee, ever since I first laid eyes on her at her potluck. I think she's very cool.

Dee and I had a fantastic time last night at La Rouche. And today I'm in such a foul mood I don't know what to do. All I write in this diary is how I'm depressed or nervous or crazy and sometimes I'm inappropriately euphoric. I should just get over myself. There are children starving in Africa. But I can't help it if I'm depressed after having a perfect evening with a beautiful woman. I mean, too bad.

Dee and I shared a bottle of wine and had French bistro food and talked about everything. She wore a simple brown dress, which directed my attention to her lovely face and sparkling eyes and newly braided hair, which was flecked with gold. I told her I was ashamed of my behavior on our first date, the way I blithered on about Terri. We laughed about my burying our pack of ciga- rettes under that bench, and Dee said, "We have to dig them up! Do you remember where they are?"

We talked about her growing up a middle-class African- American in DC. Dee said sometimes the black ladies, her mother and aunts and church-going neighbors, got on her nerves. She said they would look at a gay person, male or female, and shake their heads and go, "Mm-mm-mm."

I asked if they called lesbians "bull-daggers," and Dee laughed her head off. She said, "There's a story about that word. I never even heard it until I grew up and read some books. When I came out to my mom, she was pretty good about it, but once I got mad at her because she said she didn't want my girlfriend over at Christmas. She said, 'Honey bunch, we really want it to be just the family.' And I said, 'Oh, you're ashamed that Granny and Aunt Doris will see that your daughter is a bull-dagger!' Joanna, I'd never seen my mother so shocked. Her eyes bulged and she drew herself up and said, 'No daughter of mine will ever use that word. Ever! *Do you understand me?*' I was afraid she was going to slap me, which she'd only done twice in my life. I said, 'All right, all right!' And she went into the kitchen and refused to speak to me the whole afternoon."

"What was she so upset about?" I asked.

"She was upset that I had used a word used by low-class people. Like people in the ghetto. My mom hates people from the ghetto. She donates clothes to them and goes over to Southeast and reads to preschool children, but she hates that they drag us down. She denies it, but it's obvious. Like the girlfriend I wanted to bring over for Christmas? She was a smart-ass street girl. And she loved my mom and would bring her the nicest gifts when we went there for dinner, and my mom was as chilly to her as a gray day in November."

"Well, that's probably why she didn't want to have her for Christmas," I said.

"That and because she hadn't come to terms with my being a bull-dagger," Dee said, and we cracked up. I told Dee that my mom couldn't stand anyone who didn't speak proper English. "Both of my parents had Yiddish-speaking immigrant parents and they learned English in school," I said. "*Proper* English. If any one of us dated someone who said, 'She refused to go to the movies with him and I,' my mom wouldn't even want that person in the house. If someone said, 'She don't wanna go to the movies with him and I,' that would be the end. She would act as though the person was a member of the Aryan Brotherhood. And now her own kids use sloppy language and it drives her nuts. Like my brother Robbie will say, 'Ah, he don't know what he's doing," and my mom will said "He *doesn't* know what he's doing! My children should always speak properly!' If I say, 'That's really fucked up,' my mom will say, 'A writer should be able to choose her words more carefully.'"

"I would never say 'That's really fucked up' to my mom," Dee said.

"That's because your mom is black," I said. "You don't fuck around with black moms because they don't put up with any back-talk you hear me?"

"Oh, my mom is a potato head," Dee said irreverently because she was smashed on wine, and we laughed until I almost peed.

Dee insisted on paying for my dinner. She had the foresight to tell me not to drive, since we were going to drink, and we shared a cab home. We got to her apartment on 17th Street and then I kissed her good-night, a gentle, closed-mouthed kiss, and she smiled and got out of the cab and I went home. It was a perfect date.

And today, as I said before, I'm depressed as hell.

There's something terribly wrong with me. The only thing I'm clear about concerning my date with Dee is that it won't be a good idea to tell Kimba. I don't think she would be very supportive.

Yesterday the most extraordinary thing happened. I had decided to get a tattoo, which I had wanted ever since Kimba inked a fake "Live Free or Die" tattoo on my arm. I was walking to Tattoo Joe's on Connecticut and saw Cherry Hill gazing into an upscale boutique with a black woman with short, salt-and-pepper hair. Remembering my last sad meeting with Cherry, I was going to just keep walking, but she saw me and said, "Joanna!" in a voice more appropriate if I had been two blocks away. I stopped, and she smiled at me, and I noticed that she looked beautiful in a purple wool coat and some kicky multicolored boots. The next thing I noticed was that her companion was Judge Louise Holmes.

Judge Holmes said, "Isn't that Joanna Kane?" Cherry replied, "Yes, Louise. Staying out of trouble, I hope."

The judge laughed. "Well, I haven't seen her in my courtroom lately, so that's a good sign."

I was blown away. I knew Cherry was friends with the judge, but to see them together gave me a peculiar thrill. I had had very intense experiences with both of them, and there they were, together. "Well, hello there, ladies," I said.

"Judge Holmes, it's a pleasure to see you again, under less trying circumstances. And you'll be pleased to know I've been managing to stay out of court. But not out of trouble." I laughed.

Judge Holmes laughed too. "Joanna, I wouldn't expect you to stay out of any trouble," she said. "I just hope you're not doing anything too crazy, like lying on the ground eating sandwiches and cursing out police officers." I was practically coming in my pants that the judge remembered me and my badness so clearly. I was more turned on by that than by remembering my kinky tryst with Cherry Hill. Judge Holmes turned to Cherry and said, "Sweetie, why don't you and Joanna walk me to the Metro? I've got to be in court by four." I thought it was cute that the judge would call her friend "sweetie."

"Come on, Joanna!" Cherry ordered, as though I was their four-year-old daughter, and we walked to the Metro. Then, to my astonishment, Cherry and Judge Louse Holmes kissed each other goodbye. On the mouth. Looking into each other's eyes. I almost fell over onto the street. Then the judge stepped onto the long escalator. We watched her descend, and she turned around and gave us a coy little wave.

Cherry and I were standing there and I could barely collect myself. I stuttered that I had been on my way to get a tattoo and she said, "Fantastic! I'll go with you!" This was fine with me because I needed some explanation for what I'd just witnessed. Also I realized I could use some company during the ordeal of getting my first tattoo.

The only artist at Tattoo Joe's was busy with a client, and no one else was waiting, so Cherry and I walked around the waiting area, looking at the samples covering the walls. Finally I picked out an eagle, since I am a freedom-loving girl and also because I don't want these creepy Republicans to lay claim to our national symbols. (The eagle is softened by pastels, so it looks kind of psychedelic, and I love it.) After I made my selection, we sat down and Cherry said, "So tell me everything that's been going on with you, Joanna." I said, "No, Cherry. You tell me what's been going on with *you*."

Cherry laughed, and her laugh was still loud, but Judge Holmes must have had a civilizing effect on her because it no longer sounded like a trumpet.

"My friendship with Louise has evolved," Cherry said.

"Was she gay this whole time?" I asked, bouncing in my seat like a kid. "Was she gay when I saw her in court?"

"She was, but she wasn't out," Cherry said.

"But she's out now?"

"Yes, Joanna, she's out now!" Cherry was being patient with me. I wondered if the judge knew about our wild sex that day, but I didn't ask.

"Are you girls in love?" I said.

Cherry's face lit up like a meteor shower. "Oh, honey, we are so in love," she said. Then she whispered, but her whisper was like someone else's normal voice. "It's very physical!" she said. "We had to drag ourselves out of bed today so Louise could get to court. She's working only part-time, so we just lie in bed all day and fuck!" She laughed. I was so preoccupied by this image that I couldn't concentrate on my tattoo. I tried to re-focus. "All right, now that you know about my love life, I want to know about yours," Cherry said.

I told her that Terri had broken my heart and Dee and Terri had broken up and I had this perfect revenge date with Dee and I was totally depressed. "I think I may be mentally ill," I said.

"No, you're not," Cherry said. "You're just confused. What about that gal you were talking to at my potluck? The cute dykey one with the nice butt? I noticed something going on there, much to my chagrin."

I smiled. "You're talking about Kimba," I said. "I think she's pissed at me or something."

"Why is she pissed at you or something?"

"Well, we went out on New Year's Eve and we spent the night and made out in bed and stuff, but we're just *friends*, Cherry, except, you know, I am attracted to her, but . . ."

"You're *attracted* to her, but you're just *friends*?" Cherry yelled. "How attracted to her *are* you, Joanna?"

"Well, it's not like Terri," I said.

"Honey, Terri was your first love! That's a whole different thing! It's like the first time you go to the toilet yourself!" I looked uneasily toward the inking room, but the guy didn't came out and tell her she was ruining his concentration, and she continued roaring at me. "The first time you go to the bathroom instead of in your diaper, it's a watershed moment, if you'll excuse my choice of words. But after that first time," she continued over my laughter, "you just do it!"

"How can you compare taking a piss to falling in love?" I said.

"They're both natural physical functions!" Cherry said. "Stop glamorizing falling in love, Joanna! It's just

269

something nature dreamed up to perpetuate the species, and gay people were just created to keep the population under control." Before I had a chance to consider this intriguing theory, Cherry said, "So why did you say Kimba was angry? Or didn't you say?"

"I don't know if she is. But she's been acting funny ever since I told her that Terri called and said she and Dee were breaking up. She hasn't called me or wanted to get together very much. But I don't really think it has anything to do with that. Kimba and I are *just friends*! I don't even know why we're talking about this, to tell you the truth."

"Oh, Joanna, stop being such a child," Cherry said. "Of course Kimba was upset when you told her Terri called. And why do you think you're depressed after going out with Dee? Because, lady, you don't love Dee. I don't even think you love Terri anymore. You love Kimba! Girlfriend, you've got to stop making such a big deal out of love! Love comes and it goes. I fell in and out of love with you in about two seconds!" Before I had a chance to feel in-sulted, the door to the inner sanctum opened. "I think he's ready for you," Cherry said.

Cherry cheered me on while a huge, tattoo-slathered man named "Ranger" inked my eagle on my upper arm. It does hurt to get a tattoo, but it's better than a bellyache, which is what Kimba accused me of having after my "Live Free or Die" tattoo wore off. "Quit moaning and groaning and get a tattoo already," she said. But she wouldn't go with me because she's seen loud, brawling, ink-slathered men in blue collar bars her whole life and tattoos do not impress her.

I walked Cherry to the Metro. Before she got on the escalator, she said, "Remember, Joanna. Love is as natural as peeing. Don't hold it back, or you'll wet your pants."

A woman in her sixties getting onto the escalator said, "We wouldn't want that to happen, would we?" I didn't know if she was annoyed or amused by Cherry's pee talk, but it was pretty funny.

Cherry and I kissed goodbye and I said she was the perfect person to be present for the creation of my first tattoo. "Good luck with Louise," I said, as Cherry stepped onto the escalator. "I hope it lasts a hundred years and a day!"

Cherry looked back over her shoulder, and her face glowed in the chilly air. "Honey, if it lasts another five minutes it will have been worth it!" she called. And she kept on riding, her back erect in her purple wool coat.

The potluck group met at Dee's house again, and it was horrible.

Everyone was there, and Dee looked lovely as usual, and she had her punch fountain plugged in and the Vodka punch flowed. My tattoo was covered, but I pulled up my sleeve and showed it off and the girls oohed and aahed. Bette was there with a new girlfriend, a handsome butch with a strong build, a short haircut, and a toothy smile, and my friend was in full form to impress her sweetie, waxing eloquent about everything from the mating habits of eels to the history of underarm deodorant. Dee paid special attention to me, putting her hand on my shoulder and refreshing my drinks, and she pepped up the party with a story about her problems with the bitchy supervisor of one of her group homes.

The problem was Kimba. She wasn't paying any attention to me and, in fact, was acting kind of mean. She was strutting around, not behaving with her customary understated charm but more like a barnyard rooster, and I have to admit she looked very cute with her surfer boy hair and this silky blue shirt with some cuff links that I bought her during one of our shopping expeditions, and she had on some new jeans and new loafers and I don't even know why I noticed everything she had on, frankly, because I doubt that she noticed that I was there. Well, she did, because she blandly said that my tattoo was "nice," and then she told me to stop hogging the chips and she put me down when I said Dee's group house kids should organize a rebellion, saying, "Are you going to lead it?" I didn't appreciate her making fun of me. I didn't mean what I said literally; I was just expressing anger over the cruel inadequacies of "the system." I've always had a lot of respect for Kimba's intelligence. Not only is she one of the wittiest people I know, but she's an excellent problem-solver. She can solve any puzzle, build furniture from raw wood, install a toilet, and write impeccably (she's shown me a couple of her NASA reports and they are lucid and well-organized and not even bureaucratic-sounding). Her photography has won contests. I know all I can do is write, but she doesn't have to make me feel like an idiot when I open my mouth. I don't do that to her.

This is my problem lately. I focus on the negative. I never thought I had a negative attitude. With me, the glass was always half full. That's why I stuck with Terri for so long. If Kimba wants to be like that, so what? I can't expect my friends to be perfect. But instead of ignoring Kimba's behavior I let it bug the shit out of me while not enjoying Bette's joy over her girlfriend and Dee's sweet attentions and the vodka punch and the delicious homemade dishes and Dee's sandwich fixings with REAL mayonnaise—I'm talking about Hellman's, which is the only acceptable kind to a Jewish girl, and you know what? That's one thing that Kimba doesn't do right. She buys this ridiculous mayonnaise, I don't even remember the kind. It's some sort of off-brand shit and when I saw it in her refrigerator I screamed. She imitates me screaming, and in fact goes into this whole "Joanna" routine of my ejecting the mayonnaise from the fridge and trying to dump it in the trash, and I have to admit it's hilarious. That's another thing she does. She's a brilliant mimic. I'm a terrible mimic. I'm funny, but I'm not a good mimic.

Why am I going on and on about Kimba? Why did I let her get to me like that? I even left the potluck early, while the party was in full swing, and I walked home and those awful new tenants, the two thugs and their crack-head girlfriend, were standing in the hall when I went upstairs and I said, "Hey, kids, how ya doin'?" just to *connect* with somebody, and they looked at me as though I was a cop and one of them grunted. That happened just an hour ago and I'm thinking of tossing a Molotov cocktail in their room.

Maybe I'll call Kimba and leave a message on her answering machine. But I hate her. What am I going to say? "I hate you?" That wouldn't make me feel any better. Maybe I'll ask her if she wants to go to American City Diner for a hamburger tomorrow. I'm dying to tell her about Cherry Hill and the judge. But what if she won't go? What if she doesn't even call back?

I'll just sit here and hate myself. I can't think of anything else to do right now, except maybe go to the Reeves building and sit on the sidewalk eating a Subway sand-

274

wich. But Judge Holmes is not bothering much with her magisterial duties these days, and I would end up going before some schmuck who would make me do community service for the rest of my life.

March 2001

I've been staying at Nicky's for the past three days, waiting to see if I can move back into my burned-up building. And no, I never gave in to my urge to throw a Molotov cocktail in the street people's room. The street people wrecked the building themselves. Those morons.

Last Wednesday afternoon, the thug boys, the crack-head girl, and the two white junkie sisters tied up Gerald in the upstairs bathroom and said that if he didn't give them all his money they would set fire to the building. I had just come home and was passing the bathroom and the door was closed, and I heard Gerald yell in his queeny voice, "Don't you understand? My money is tied up!" And one of the thugs said, "No, YOU are tied up!" and Gerald said, "I mean I don't have any liquid assets," and I heard the crackhead girl scream, "Shut up, motherfucker! We don't care about your liquid asses! Just tell us where the money is!" Then I heard one of the junkie girls say, "Yeah, we need it to send to our families," and her sister said, "Hush, Joleen." I was standing there, wondering what the hell to do. Then Gerald said, "Please put that gasoline can away and untie me. We'll work something out."

And the second thug said, "Fuck all that! Tell us where your bank card or money is or we turn you into toast."

I ran to Jerome's room and found him lying placidly on his bed. "Those scumbags have tied up Gerald in the bathroom and are trying to rob him!" I yelled. "They're threatening to burn down the building!"

"I got nothin' to do with those fools," Jerome said, looking at the TV instead of me. I realized with a shock that he had probably masterminded the whole thing. "I'm gonna call the cops," I said. "Those people are desperate. What if they set fire to the building and we all burn up?"

"There's a fire escape right outside," Jerome said. "We ain't gonna burn up. Anyway, they ain't gonna set no fire."

"How do you know?"

"'Cause they ain't." He probably told them to just use the gasoline can to threaten Gerald. But then I heard a splashing sound and ran out and saw one of the white girls pouring gasoline over the carpet. "What the fuck are you doing?" I screamed. Jerome got up off his bed as though he was responding to a call to dinner and went into the hall. "What I tell you?" he said. He walked up to the junkie and pulled the gas can out of her hands. "Fuck you, Jerome!" she said. Jerome went to the bathroom and I trotted behind. We found the two thugs, the crackhead, and the second white girl in there with poor Gerald, who was lying on his back in the bathtub, all tied up with rope.

"You son-of-a-bitch!" screamed Gerald. "How can you do this to me?"

"Y'all shouldn't have thrown me out," Jerome said. I wasn't aware that Gerald had evicted Jerome, who seemed to have a steady supply of income, but then Jerome said, "You know you liked it."

"You were having sex with *Gerald?*" I said.

"Oh, yes," Jerome drawled with a hint of a smile. "The boy had the time of his life."

"God!" I said. "You fuck Gerald right on top of fucking Nicky and the whole rest of the world? You're unbelievable."

"Nicky is my heart," Jerome said. "Gerald is my slave boy."

"I hate you, Jerome!" Gerald shrieked. "You are a horrible man! I want you to untie me this instant!"

"Shut up, motherfucker!" the crackhead said.

"Be quiet, Tee Tee," said one of the thugs, and looked at Jerome for instructions.

"Untie him," Jerome said, and one of the thugs started to untie the knots that bound Gerald, and suddenly there was a woosh! The hallway was on fire, and the junkie girl came to the bathroom door with a grin on her face, and I realized that she was demented. "Burn, house! Burn, house! Burn, burn, burn!" she yelled, waving a book of matches. Fortunately there was a fire escape outside the bathroom, and we all got out of there, including Gerald, who wasn't tied very securely. The junkie fire setter didn't want to go and her sister pleaded with her, "Come on, Joleen, come *on!*", but Joleen just stood there with that crazy grin and the sister screamed, "She's mental, she doesn't know what she's doing," and finally Jerome picked her up and carried her like a sack of potatoes onto the fire escape and pushed her down ahead of him.

We were the only ones on the second floor of the

house, and everyone on the first floor got out safely. It was a miracle that no one was hurt or killed. Thank God Johnny and Guillermo were out visiting Guillermo's family in Wheaton. The fire department came immediately, but the second floor of the building was extensively damaged. My place, which was at the corner of the hall, was intact except for some smoke damage, but the smell in there was pretty bad.

Nicky insisted that I stay with him in his beautiful brick two-story house on upper 16th Street. Nicky has been living by himself ever since his veterinarian boyfriend left and said he hates living alone and he gave me the whole second floor, which he never uses. Jerome has come here a couple times and banged on the door and begged Nicky to let him in so he could "explain what happened," and Nicky refuses to let him in, but then he goes into his room and cries. Then he comes out and pops a couple of his headache pills.

I know Nicky can use a good friend and I should have moved in with him months ago, when the all those street people started appearing in the building. But I can't let go of anything. I get attached to people and places and even after they go bad I cling to them for dear life. I'm one of those Jews who would have refused to leave Nazi Germany. I would have been running around yelling, "Visa, Schmeeza! I'm not going anywhere! My family has been here for 200 years! Don't listen to Uncle Moishe with his crazy stories! Someone dropped him on his head when he was three years old!" On and on, all the way to the showers.

March in DC, and spring has come in like a lamb. I'm out of the building for good, because Gerald is repairing it and then selling it and moving to Australia to become a ranch hand. I laughed when I heard that, but somehow it seemed right. After his humiliation in the bathtub, Gerald is going to reclaim his manhood. I wish him all the best.

On Sunday, movers are going to transport my stuff here to Nicky's. Dr. Bobb said maybe I should store it and give Nicky some time to know if he really wants me to stay, but Nicky said not to listen to "that crazy man" (spoken with sugary affection), and insisted that I stay here as long as I want.

Yesterday Kimba called and Nicky told her what happened and she came over with a big bowl of homemade spaghetti. She hugged me and said she's so, so sorry. The three of us ate dinner and then we played scrabble in Nicky's cozy living room. Afterwards Nicky went into his room to call his friends and Kimba and I went out on his porch, where it was warm and breezy. Kimba and I sat on the swing, and I put my arm around her, and we listened to the rustle of the trees and the cars going by.

"Were you pissed at me?" I asked.

"Yes," she said.

"Why?" I asked.

"You didn't ask me to go out with you after New Year's Eve," she said.

"I did," I said. Then I remembered. "Well, I was going to. But then Terri called and I told you, and you seemed so irritated, and then *you* didn't call *me*."

"I heard you went out with Dee."

"Did you not want me to go out with Dee?"

Kimba looked at me, her face about an inch from mine. "I did not want you to go out with Dee," she said. I thought she was going to kiss me, but she didn't. She just turned away and kept looking out onto the leafy, light-splashed street.

April 2001

I'm happy because I love Kimba. Do you have to love someone to be happy? I know that loving someone doesn't *make* you happy. I wasn't happy when I loved Terri because she didn't love me. But Kimba loves me. She collects things from the woods and gives them to me. She bought me a necklace and a bicycle. She cooks spaghetti and meatballs for me and she baked a cherry pie for me, Billy boy, Billy boy. She smells like apricots. She makes me laugh all day long.

We laugh while we're having sex. Is that normal? I never laughed while having sex, except with Cherry Hill, when we played nurse-patient. But I laugh harder with Kimba, even when I'm coming. She indulges me in this Judge Holmes sex game, in which she "does" Judge Holmes, ordering me to do this or that, and it's amazing how accurate her imitation is considering that she's never even met Louise. I have a better time with Kimba than I've ever had with anyone in my life.

Nicky said I should consider this place my home. He said there's plenty of room and even if he gets a boy-friend I can still live here. I'm paying the same rent that

I paid Gerald for a large bedroom, a smaller room that I use for reading and writing, and a bathroom. The bedroom has an upper porch, which overlooks beautiful 16th Street. The late-afternoon sun splashes in around the time that I go to work, and in the morning I can enjoy the sunny back patio, which faces east. Nicky and I share the kitchen and living room, and he has his own large bedroom and a study where he often does his legal work, which he's trying to catch up on since all the distractions of the past few months.

It's nice that Kimba and Nicky are friends, because he heartily approves of her staying over here on weekends. (I spend a couple nights over at her place during the week, because she has to get up early on weekdays.) Kimba is turning me into a pig with her big breakfasts—eggs and sausage and English muffins and sometimes she even throws in a steak.

I took Kimba to see Dr. Bobb and he was almost as excited as when he sees Nicky and gave her a hug. "You have no idea how thrilled I am that you have rescued Joanna," he said. Willi, my friend and ex-therapist, would think Dr. Bobb is absurd to say that someone "rescued" me instead of that I *chose* to be with her. But I suppose you can choose to be rescued. Kimba asked Dr. Bobb to show her his top, and he pulled it out of the drawer, and they both played with it. Kimba loves to play. She likes to shoot pool and play Frisbee and poker and basketball. She soon got the hang of Dr. Bobb's top and was shooting it higher than he ever got it and he said, "You bitch," and she smiled, and I said, "What kind of therapist calls his patient's lover a bitch? It's very unprofessional." I said to

Kimba, "Dr. Bobb and Nicky are in love with each other," and Kimba said, "I've heard." Dr. Bobb said, "It's the purist of Platonic loves. I am hopelessly heterosexual." And I said, "But you don't have a girlfriend. We have to find you a girlfriend." Dr. Bobb said, "I keep telling you that, but what have you done about it? After all I've done for you, your failure to produce a suitable woman for me is inexcusable."

On Friday, Kimba and I took personal days and Nicky finished some work at home and we decided to go to Rock Creek Park and fly Kimba's kite. We got in Nicky's Jaguar and Nicky said, "Let's go get Bob Bobb. Maybe he'll come with us." Nicky's still mourning Jerome, so to make him happy we went down to Dr. Bobb's office. He had just finished with his last patient and said he would be delighted to go with us. We drove to the park, singing to oldies on the radio, and we traipsed to a soccer field and we gave Dr. Bobb the kite. He got the string tangled up and Kimba had to untangle it for him, and then the kite fluttered up and crashed to the ground, and Kimba instructed Dr. Bobb to turn around so the kite would fly in the direction of the wind, and finally the kite went up and we all gazed up at it. "I never flew a kite before," Dr. Bobb said. "In Jamaica they put you in jail for kite-flying."

"Oh, baloney," I said. "They did not. You just weren't cool enough to fly kites in Jamaica, so you make up a story that they put you in jail for it."

"Well, that's true," Dr. Bobb said. "But they handed out very stiff fines for kite flying in Jamaica."

"He lies like a rug," Nicky said to Kimba. "You can't believe a word of what he says. He's clinically insane."

"But he cures people," I said. "That's the scary thing about it."

"I cure people because I care about them," Dr. Bobb said. "And because I help them to liberate their life force.

"Aooow!" I howled, as the wind got hole of the kite and it fluttered in the sky. When I looked up at the kite, I saw how beautiful it was. It was a silver, orange, and green box kite with a long tail. "Where'd you get that kite, honey?" I asked Kimba.

"I made it," she said.

"You made it?"

"Yes."

"When did you make it?" I figured she had made it back when she was in school, for an art project or something.

"I made it last week," Kimba said. "I've always wanted to make a kite."

It occurred to me that she made the kite so we could both fly it. I went over and hugged her.

"You see?" Dr. Bobb said, as he unraveled more string to make the kite go higher. "You found the right girl. She's an artist, like you."

Terri and I had lunch today down at the Afterwards Café in Dupont Circle. She's seeing some woman, but she doesn't like her much. I was glad that she wasn't all la-la-la in love. I'm not in love with Terri anymore, but seeing her sitting there at the table I felt as though I'd come home, just as I did when I ran into her last week at the Cherry Blossom Festival. I couldn't say no when she asked me out for lunch. I don't like to toss people out of my life. I even kind of miss that crazy man Jerome, even though I won't touch him with a ten-foot pole because he would use me to get to Nicky.

Dr. Bobb said I was crazy to make a lunch date with Terri. He said, "She treated you like shit and you're making nice with her? What are you, a wimp? Little wimpy Joanna, having lunch with the woman who broke her heart. I suppose you'll pay for the lunch too." But as a black man he should know what it's about. It's a tribal thing.

Years ago I read a book called *The Gypsies,* an autobiographical account of a boy who ran away from his middle-class Swedish home back in the thirties and joined a tribe of Gypsies. Once, when his adopted family made camp, a caravan of gypsy slobs showed up. The author's family, who maintained high standards of behavior and hygiene, was disgusted by these newcomers, who were infested with scabies and trashed the camp and dumped their waste downstream, polluting the water. But the family tolerated these lowlifes because they were gypsies. They were "family." It's like Robert Frost's observation that "home" is the place where, when you go there, they have to take you in.

Perhaps I shouldn't compare an unkempt gypsy family with Terri, who showers every day and keeps her waste separate from her drinking water. But like the gypsies, we're "family." We're in the same tribe. And I realize now that, even though she wasn't so nice to me, she had her reasons. When I met Terri, she was still mourning the only woman she'd ever loved, and then her mother died, and I was there mooning over her. She wanted to love me, but she couldn't. I was too nuts. She wanted a more grounded woman, someone who'd been around the block a few times, not a 45-year-old teenager. Not that it excused her insensitivity to me, but I wasn't exactly sensitive to a lot of the men who fell for me. I used some of them the way Terri used me.

I loved her. Everyone said I was obsessed, and maybe I was, but I also loved her. I'm not talking about at the beginning, when I fell in love with her. "In love" is a misnomer that has nothing to do with love. I'm talking about after she broke my heart. Strangely, that's when I got to love her, because that's when I got to *know* her. She was a little shit at times, but I still loved her. I loved her because she was a sassy Jewish girl from Cleveland, Ohio. Because she tried to win love through achievements. Because she hid her vulnerability behind layers of attitude. Because underneath her forced charm she was an angry, lonely child. I loved her because she was me.

Kimba encouraged me to have lunch with Terri. She understands about these things. In fact, tomorrow she's having lunch with her ex, who broke her heart almost as badly as Terri broke mine. And then next week we're having a Cinco de Mayo party at Kimba's and we're inviting both of them. I don't want to invite Terri because she'll distract me and I still hate her with all my holy talk about forgiving her. But I'm doing it anyway because I'm used to cooking myself up into a stew. With all my improvement, I'm still hard-wired for stress.

Dr. Bobb wants to use me as a guinea pig for a machine he's building in his basement. He said it alters the hard-wiring in your brain, and as soon as he irons out the kinks he will try it on me.

"Are you going to try it on yourself?" I asked.

"Not on your life," he said. "Do you think I'm out of my mind?"

"Well, then, why do you want to use it on me?" I yelled.

"Because you *are* out of your mind," he said.

Maybe I am. But so is everyone else in this town, including him. What an adventure this has been. Sometimes I still feel crazy, in spite of my happiness, because who can be sane in Washington, DC? It's in a different dimension from everywhere else. I may as well be living in Oz. One day the city is shimmering with color and life and everyone's skipping down the yellow brick road and the next day it's as overcast and ominous as the sky where the flying monkeys sped on their evil errands. Today, in the spring of 2001, the first official year of the new Millennium, the city is shimmering with color and life.

I wish I could stop time.

Lisa Gitlin

Lisa Gitlin grew up in Cleveland, Ohio. Her father was a newspaperman and she always knew she wanted to be a writer. When she reached adolescence she realized she was attracted to girls, and in order to distract herself from her forbidden longings she engaged in a lot of mischief. She settled down in high school, had lots of rebellious fun at Ohio State University, and after three years moved to New York City. She was enchanted by New York's rough edges and stayed in the city long enough to write a lot of poems and short stories and complete college at the New School for Social Research (now the New School for General Studies). Eventually she ended up back in Cleveland, where she forged a long free-lance writing career and was published in many local and national publications. Finally, in her forties, she came out with a big bang, fell madly in love, and moved to Washington DC. She plans to move back to New York City one day.

Acknowledgments

I could not have written this book without the love and support of the following people:

My wonderful family:

Mom—I'll sing the Friday song any time you want—You are the best mom ever!

Thanks to my sister Queen—for enriching my life with her love, sweetness and humor. Thanks also to Kathy, my sweet and salty big sis; brother Bobby (Crunchy)—my true hero; and brother Marty (Ginch)—(maybe it *is* a get-together!). Thanks to Barb, David, Mitzi for loving them and me. To my charming niece Emily who loves pink, and my wild niece Melanie, aka "Search and Destroy"—you both fill me with joy. To Auntie who loves me no matter what, and to all my cool cousins. Bobie and Zadie, your love endures inside of me.

My fantastic friends:

Thanks to Klo—my best friend—you'll always be a part of me (but I know our birthdays are separate). Rogey, I would be a quivering mass of jelly without you. Click, you are one of the main "peeps" I speak for! Boy—my soulmate—we'll travel through time together. T—IKIN2BDP. Lortie—you're my bush peppy brother—love you endlessly. Love you too, Ben! Thanks to Els and Mortie and Jockey and Kathy C—old friends who nourish my spirit.

And to my beloved DC/MD friends: TiVo, guess who's my REAL BFF? Dood, you're the best "lagniappe!" a girl could ever ask for! Kaboo-die! Thanks for being "you." Jubee—you own a piece of my heart duh-uh! Puck you rock girl love you lots. T.C. and Margaret and Puddin' and Kaye, Norma and Linda—you are true and loyal friends. Thanks to my dear Shabbat girls—"Peaceful" Annie (smile), buzzin' Bethany, Kati the Hungarian spitfire, smart and sassy Cindi, and Judy the New York latke queen—you are all the greatest. Romie—you're a true kindred spirit.

Reverend P.—thanks for being a good sport. You know I love you.

Shirley—thanks for enduring the trials of Job.

Special thanks to my readers: Kati and Tivo, you opened my eyes—Jubee and Puddin', thanks for helping me fine-tune, thanks also to Edie Harriet, and most of all, thanks to brother Robert, fellow writer and staunchest critic—when you gave your thumbs up all was well.

Shout-out to my special kids—Sammy, who delights

me with his energy and humor, my scintillating god-daughter Olympia, who fills me with pride, and dear Sophie, whose loving spirit sweetens the world— Thank you all for lighting up my life.

Thank you to Bywater Books for having faith in my "baby!"—You have made possible the best moment of my life. Thanks to Marianne for your support, wisdom, and empathy, and to Kelly, for your commitment to my book, editorial astuteness, and respect for me as a writer—I'm happy and proud to be a member of the "Bywater family"!

And finally—Sydney—I don't have to say it because you know everything.

Love and thanks to you all—
Lisa

Bywater Books represents the coming of age of lesbian fiction. We're committed to bringing the best of contemporary lesbian writing to a discerning readership. Our editorial team is dedicated to finding and developing outstanding voices who deliver stories you won't want to put down. That's why we sponsor the annual Bywater Prize. We love good books, just like you do.

For more information about Bywater Books and the annual *Bywater Prize for Fiction*, please visit our website.

www.bywaterbooks.com